GIRL NINE: GONE

(A Maya Gray Mystery—Book 9)

Molly Black

Molly Black

Bestselling author Molly Black is author of the MAYA GRAY FBI suspense thriller series, comprising nine books; of the RYLIE WOLF FBI suspense thriller series, comprising six books; of the TAYLOR SAGE FBI suspense thriller series, comprising eight books; of the KATIE WINTER FBI suspense thriller series, comprising eleven books (and counting); of the RUBY HUNTER FBI suspense thriller series, comprising five books (and counting); of the CAITLIN DARE FBI suspense thriller series, comprising five books (and counting); of the REESE LINK mystery series, comprising five books (and counting); and of the CLAIRE KING mystery series, comprising five books (and counting).

An avid reader and lifelong fan of the mystery and thriller genres, Molly loves to hear from you, so please feel free to visit www.mollyblackauthor.com to learn more and stay in touch.

ISBN: 978-1-0943-7913-5

BOOKS BY MOLLY BLACK

MAYA GRAY MYSTERY SERIES
GIRL ONE: MURDER (Book #1)
GIRL TWO: TAKEN (Book #2)
GIRL THREE: TRAPPED (Book #3)
GIRL FOUR: LURED (Book #4)
GIRL FIVE: BOUND (Book #5)
GIRL SIX: FORSAKEN (Book #6)
GIRL SEVEN: CRAVED (Book #7)
GIRL EIGHT: HUNTED (Book #8)
GIRL NINE: GONE (Book #9)

RYLIE WOLF FBI SUSPENSE THRILLER
FOUND YOU (Book #1)
CAUGHT YOU (Book #2)
SEE YOU (Book #3)
WANT YOU (Book #4)
TAKE YOU (Book #5)
DARE YOU (Book #6)

TAYLOR SAGE FBI SUSPENSE THRILLER
DON'T LOOK (Book #1)
DON'T BREATHE (Book #2)
DON'T RUN (Book #3)
DON'T FLINCH (Book #4)
DON'T REMEMBER (Book #5)
DON'T TELL (Book #6)

KATIE WINTER FBI SUSPENSE THRILLER
SAVE ME (Book #1)
REACH ME (Book #2)
HIDE ME (Book #3)
BELIEVE ME (Book #4)

HELP ME (Book #5)
FORGET ME (Book #6)
HOLD ME (Book #7)
PROTECT ME (Book #8)
REMEMBER ME (Book #9)
CATCH ME (Book #10)
WATCH ME (Book #11)

RUBY HUNTER FBI SUSPENSE THRILLER
IF I RUN (Book #1)
IF I TELL (Book #2)
IF I LIVE (Book #3)
IF I FORGET (Book #4)
IF I RETURN (Book #5)

CAITLIN DARE FBI SUSPENSE THRILLER
COME GET ME (Book #1)
COME FIND ME (Book #2)
COME TAKE ME (Book #3)
COME CATCH ME (Book #4)
COME SAVE ME (Book #5)

REESE LINK MYSTERY
BEYOND REASON (Book #1)
BEYOND REACH (Book #2)
BEYOND REPAIR (Book #3)
BEYOND DOUBT (Book #4)
BEYOND NORMAL (Book #5)

CLAIRE KING MYSTERY
ONCE HE SEES (Book #1)
ONCE HE LONGS (Book #2)
ONCE HE TAKES (Book #3)
ONCE HE FEELS (Book #4)
ONCE HE KNOWS (Book #5)

CHAPTER ONE

Bret didn't mind working his beat in the Three Hills area of Chesterford. It was one of the better parts of the town, with a few good restaurants and a smattering of expensive bars and galleries. It was the kind of place where his main job was to be out there, to be seen, and to occasionally deal with a complaint about a stolen wallet.

Bret was grateful for that. He was still pretty new on the force, still getting used to what it meant to be a cop in a town like this. He still had the excitement that came with now being a fully-fledged member of the CPD, mixed with a sense of responsibility, because now the things he said and did could have a huge impact on people's lives.

Bret was walking up South Street, the main strip as far as this part of town was concerned, taking it slow, not in a hurry. Around here, a big part of his job was simply to be seen, so that the rich folks felt that they were getting their tax dollars' worth from the local police department. Bret kept a careful eye out for petty criminals and potential problems as he went. A part of him even wanted there to be trouble, just so he would have more of a chance to prove himself.

For now, though, it looked like a boring night, with no chance of—

"Officer Sorenson, this is Control."

Bret grabbed for his radio. He should have known better. "Go ahead, Control."

"We've had a tip just called in about a disturbance near your location."

"Where?" Bret asked.

"Hillside Park, just past the bandstand."

At this time of night, the park would be mostly deserted, but that just made it exactly the kind of place where addicts or the homeless might gather. It was probably nothing, but Bret knew he needed to check it out.

"I'm on my way."

He hurried off in the direction of the park. It was just a block over, but even so, it was like stepping into a different world as he passed from a space lit by streetlights and the neon displays of bars to one where the only real light was that of the slowly waxing moon.

Bret hurried in through the gates of the park, heading for the old bandstand. He had his flashlight out now, sweeping the area around him for trouble, the beam illuminating the branches of some of the park's trees as they rustled in the wind. Bret didn't check the service weapon he had by his side, because he didn't want to go reaching for it every time he felt nervous, but it was an effort of will not to.

Bret looked around, trying to find the disturbance that had been called in. There was no sign of anyone there, no sign of anything happening. Bret started to reach for his radio, ready to call in that it was a false alarm.

Then he saw a dark shape ahead, lit by the moonlight. Was there someone there, standing near the bandstand?

"Who's there?" Bret demanded, continuing to move forward. "Identify yourself! This is the police!"

He half-expected the figure to turn and run, not wanting the police to find out what they were doing there at this time of night. If they did, then should he run after them or just let them go?

It was a quiet night and Bret was eager to prove himself. Of course he was going to run after them.

Yet they *didn't* run. Instead, they stood still, holding position in an almost unnatural way. Bret didn't like that, didn't like it at all. He *really* didn't like it here, in this empty place, with the cold silver of the moonlight shining down.

Bret kept moving forward. He had to; he was a cop. He *did* draw his gun now, trying to be ready for whatever this turned out to be, however dangerous the situation was. He kept the beam of his flashlight pointed at the figure, trying to make out what was going on there.

As he got closer, Bret stopped and simply stared, horrified at the sight of what was in front of him.

A woman was there, standing up, tied in place against a post that seemed designed to keep her precisely in that one spot. Her blonde hair fell forward over her face, obscuring her features, while she wore a pale dress that billowed slightly as the wind caught it. Tied there as she was, the moonlight threw a shadow down like a finger reaching out toward Bret.

A dark stain was spread across the front of the woman's dress, and for a moment, Bret's mind refused to acknowledge what it was. As the reality of it started to sink in, Bret found his heart beating faster and his breath coming in short gasps. He put his gun away and moved forward, reaching out with one shaking hand to test for a pulse.

Bret recoiled from the cold, still form, staggering back, trying to fight the urge to throw up. He knew that he couldn't, that he had to preserve the crime scene, that he had to check the area for threats.

He knew all the things that he ought to do, but with a dead body in front of him, it was hard to keep his composure well enough to do any of it. Bret found himself staring at the body, his mouth opening and closing with no sound coming out.

Finally, he grabbed for his radio.

"Control, I need backup. Lots of backup." He knew he didn't sound the way a police officer should, but he didn't care right then. All that mattered was getting help and not having to be the one to deal with all of this. "There… there's a body here."

"Can you repeat that, Officer Sorenson?"

"There's a body!" Bret shouted into the radio. "Someone… someone's been murdered!"

CHAPTER TWO

Maya lay in her hospital room, trying and failing to shut out the sound of her boss shouting at her.

"You've gone too far this time, Grey!" Maya's boss, Deputy Director Harris, stood over her bed, shaven headed, wearing a dark suit and currently so angry that it had turned his normally pale features beet-red.

Maya wasn't in any mood for this. She wanted to be out there, chasing after the Moonlight Killer and her sister. Maya had succeeded in finding the spot where he was keeping the hostages he'd used to force her into working the cases he wanted. She'd managed to free all of the hostages except her sister, but the Moonlight Killer had escaped, taking Megan with him.

"I'll have your job for this," Harris promised her. "No, I'll have you thrown in *jail* for this!"

Maya ached too much to put up with Harris and his threats. She was still recovering from the shot the Moonlight Killer had winged her with as the two of them had tried to kill one another down in his bunker. She still hurt from the fight they'd had there. She could only imagine what she looked like right then, tall frame encased in a hospital gown, dark hair falling in a tangled mess, still with a few flecks of blood and ash in it from the night before. To Harris, she must look weak.

Maya hated that.

"For what?" she demanded. "For successfully freeing three hostages? For trying to take down a kidnapper?"

Maya knew how much trouble she was in for all of this, but that didn't mean that she was going to go down without a fight.

"For going rogue," Harris shot back. "You went off without telling anyone to try to take down the Moonlight Killer. You aren't the head of a task force anymore, Agent Grey. You don't get to make up your own cases."

"You told me that the task force was being shut down as of this morning," Maya replied. She hated having to hide behind such a thin distinction, but right then, it was all she had. "That means that last night, I still had the authority to act alone."

That didn't make Harris look any happier. "You're on thin ice with this, Grey. No. You *were* on thin ice. Now, you seem to have been determined to stomp your way through it and plunge into the water below. You *know* that I didn't want you to do anything else without informing me."

"With respect, sir, what I know is you told me that, as of this morning, my task force was being folded into Agent Swift's one that's hunting for the Moonlight Killer."

Harris gave a kind of angry snort then. "So you thought you would go off alone, try to take down the Moonlight Killer, lose him and burn down the evidence that might have led us to him?"

"*He* burned down the bunker," Maya said. "He set charges there and detonated them to give himself time to escape. I could have gone after him, but that would have meant abandoning three women to burn to death."

"And how many more will the Moonlight Killer murder when he's still out there?" Harris asked. It seemed obvious what decision he would have made if he'd been there on the ground.

"And *that's* why I didn't keep you in the loop on this," Maya snapped. She knew she shouldn't speak that way to her boss, but right then she was in too much pain to care. She was probably going to lose her job over all of this anyway, and her sister was still in the hands of a serial killer, so why should she hold back?

"Careful, Agent Grey."

"If *you'd* been more careful, I wouldn't have had to do all of this alone. You've spent this whole kidnapping case trying to charge in after the kidnapper, putting the lives of his hostages at risk. I knew that if you found out this was the Moonlight Killer, you would have done anything to catch him, regardless of how many people got killed."

Harris took a step back. "You're out of line, Grey. You've been out of line since the start of this. You think that because your sister is caught up in this, you're the only one who can do anything about it. Well, I'm calling an inquiry board to look into your actions."

That hurt, especially after everything Maya had done.

"My actions have seen multiple women released from the clutches of a kidnapper," Maya said. "They've also gotten us closer than anything in the last few years to catching the Moonlight Killer."

"And you *lost* him," Harris snapped back. "You took a chance and you failed. Now it's time to pay the price for that. As soon as they release you from here, I want you back in the office for your inquiry panel. You're done, Grey."

He turned and walked out, not giving Maya a chance to reply.

Maya wanted to get up and punch something. She wanted to go after Harris and… well, if she was probably going to be fired and maybe even arrested anyway, she might as well get in one good punch for all the times he'd put her sister's life in danger. Maya reminded herself that her sister's life was the only part of this that mattered. If she got arrested for hitting Harris, she wouldn't be in a position to try to get Megan back.

Maya got up, ignoring the pain in her side. There were bandages there now as she stripped off the hospital gown, getting dressed in her own clothes. Maya was just finishing up when there was a knock on the door and Marco entered.

He was in his street clothes. He'd clearly been released from the hospital, but he was still moving a little stiffly. His normally athletic swimmer's body seemed a little more fragile than usual. His sandy hair was as disheveled as ever, but the fading bruises still showed on his face from where he'd been attacked by someone sent by the Moonlight Killer to ensure that he couldn't take part in their previous case. He headed over to Maya, taking her in his arms, holding her there for several seconds.

"You should have told me where you were going."

It was very different from when Harris had been insisting on the same thing. Harris had done nothing but make life more difficult for Maya as she'd tried to investigate this case. Marco had been there for Maya, both personally and professionally. He'd been a partner to her, but he'd become so much more as well.

"I couldn't risk anyone overhearing it."

"And you knew I'd try to talk you out of it?" Marco suggested. "You went to take on the Moonlight Killer alone, in his bunker, without any backup. You could have been killed, Maya."

Maya nodded. "I had to do this. I had one chance. I couldn't risk bringing any backup but you."

"And I was out of commission." Marco sounded angry about that, like he should have been there.

"The Moonlight Killer made *sure* you couldn't be there." Maya hated that she'd been manipulated like that. The Moonlight Killer had found out that she would be coming, had tried to kill her as she arrived to try to capture him.

"And now he's escaped, with your sister," Marco said.

Maya nodded, barely able to contain the hurt she felt at the memory of the Moonlight Killer running out into the night with Megan. Having to turn back to save the other hostages had been one of the most painful experiences of Maya's life, but she'd had no choice.

"I have to get her back, Marco," Maya said.

"You will." Marco sounded confident but Maya could hear the note of worry underneath that.

He didn't need to say how dangerous the situation had just become. Maya had tried to capture the Moonlight Killer and failed, leaving her sister in his hands. For all she knew, Megan might already be dead, murdered in retaliation for Maya's attempt to end all of this.

"He's going to kill her," Maya said. "If I don't find a way to get to Megan first, he's going to kill her."

Marco put a reassuring hand on her shoulder. "We'll find a way to get to her."

"How?" That was the problem. "I found his bunker. I found him and the hostages. But any evidence there is burned. Or most of it will be. Maybe the techs will be able to get something from it, but it won't be enough. This is someone who is former special ops. He'll be able to disappear if he wants to. That would even be the smart move for him."

Which was a horrifying thought. If Maya were the Moonlight Killer, if she were being a coldly logical psychopath, wouldn't that be exactly what she would do? Wouldn't she decide that it was all over, kill the last remaining connection tying her to all of it, and disappear?

Maya had to hold back tears at the thought of Megan being dead. Dead because of her. Dead because of some dangerous game that she hadn't been given any choice about playing.

"Can he just walk away, though?" Marco asked.

That question hit Maya like a punch to the gut. Marco was right; she'd been thinking about this all wrong. How long had she spent now looking for the Moonlight Killer? Weeks at least. In that time, she hadn't been able to find out much about who he was, but she *had* gotten to understand something about the way his mind worked.

He was highly intelligent, driven, capable. He was a psychopath who would do whatever it took to achieve his aims. But those aims didn't seem to waver. He was obsessive. He'd gone to extreme lengths to draw Maya into all of this.

He had a plan, and he wasn't going to deviate from that. Whatever he was trying to do, he would have to try to complete it, wouldn't he? He wouldn't be able to simply walk away.

Maya had to hope that was true. She had to trust that the Moonlight Killer's need to finish the project he'd started would override everything else: his need to stay safe, his worries that Maya was closing in, all of it. Maybe there was a way to use that to get her sister back, even now.

"We can still do this," Maya said. "We can still bring Megan back, catch the Moonlight Killer, all of it."

She had to believe that.

"What about all the stuff with the task force being shut down?" Marco asked. "Even if we aren't fired, will Agent Swift let us go after him?"

Agent Swift ran the task force that had been hunting for the Moonlight Killer ever since his killing spree began. She had been suspicious of Maya ever since she'd started to suspect that the Moonlight Killer and the kidnapper were the same person.

That didn't matter though, not right then.

"I have to do this, Marco," Maya said. "You know that Megan won't be safe with Harris, or even Swift, running all of this. I'll do whatever I need to do to get her back."

Even if it meant doing this outside the FBI.

"It won't come to that," Marco said. "But if it does, I'll be there. I started helping you out because I wanted to catch this guy, and I kept going because I believe in you, Maya. And… well, because of everything I feel about you."

Maya leaned closer to kiss him. "I feel the same way."

"Should you really be out of bed, though?" Marco asked. "Are you really ready to leave?"

"I have to be," Maya said. "I have to get Megan back. First, though, I have to go back to the FBI."

"I saw Harris leaving. I take it that it's not good?"

Maya shook her head. "He's pulling together an inquiry board. He wants to know about everything that I've done on this case. He's threatened to fire me, maybe even arrest me."

"*Could* he arrest you?" Marco asked, sounding concerned.

He had to know the answer to that. They'd held back evidence, deceived Harris and the rest of the FBI. The only protection Maya had was that she'd been in charge of her own task force, free to act the way she wanted on the case.

"If they spin it that I've gone rogue? I don't know for sure. It could go either way."

"Whatever happens, I'll be there," Marco said.

Maya was grateful for that. They had to face up to this together.

CHAPTER THREE

The man they called Frank drove, trying to contain his anger. That anger felt like a shard of ice inside his heart. His gloved hands gripped the wheel tightly, while a mask sat on the passenger seat next to him, leaving good-looking, square-jawed features uncovered.

He drove along rural trackways, staying off the main highways where traffic cameras might pick up his features or his car. There was no reason to believe that Maya had details of either, but he knew now that he needed to be careful. She had already proven to be even more resourceful than he'd anticipated.

That was a big part of what made him angry.

Angry enough that he wanted to stop the car, pull Megan Grey from the trunk where he'd stashed her, and kill her, just to try to assuage the frozen shard of fury that was there inside him.

Some version of it had always been in him. It had been there when he'd been in the military, turning him into an efficient killer, a deadly weapon to be pointed in the direction of the enemy.

It had been there when he left. All that fury because he couldn't seem to change what he was. Because he'd taken away all that potential from others. He'd seen then what he was, and what he had to be.

He'd started to find his victims then, poised on the edge of transformation, balanced on the very edge of change. He'd killed them under the full moon, the way he'd been trained to kill. He'd killed them at the moment of transformation, taking that potential each time.

Frank brought the car to a halt, the same cold fury inside him. He actually got out, standing by it, standing there next to the trunk, a length of rope in his hand. He was ready to open it and end this, there and then.

Logic dictated that he should. Even the logic of his game. Maya had broken the rules that he'd set out, and there should be consequences for that. He *should* take Megan out, strangle her and leave her body for her sister to find. He should make her pay for that. He could already imagine the pain that would cause her. Caring was her weakness, and he could hurt her now more than she'd ever been hurt before.

He could disappear then, admit that this was over, go back to his other work and leave the business of forcing Maya to clarify what he had and hadn't done alone. In any case, Frank imagined that the FBI would want to look through all the old cases attributed to him, now that they understood what he'd been doing.

All his training said that he should do this. You struck hard, you struck fast. You completed the mission and then you disappeared.

That was the problem, though, he *wasn't* done. He had set things up to reveal the pattern of his kills, to take away the detritus, to make it clear who he *had* killed, and why. That work wasn't done. He'd planned to strip away a dozen blemishes against his name.

Twelve of anything was important. Completing things was important.

Frank forced himself to get back in the car, driving deeper off the beaten track to a location that he'd picked out as a bolt hole, a backup. It was important to have such places ready, important to plan for contingencies.

His bolt hole in this case was an old farmhouse just a little way from a broad patch of woodland. The kind of place that a man might settle down in his retirement. The kind of place where a man might see his enemies coming.

Frank took Megan out of the trunk, tying her to a tree. He didn't bother with the mask now. The way this ended, either she and her sister would be dead, or Frank would. There was no more need for secrets now.

Megan stared at him in obvious terror. She'd clearly worked out what seeing his face meant. Frank put a reassuring hand on her shoulder.

"Not yet. Not until this is all finished."

He left her there while he went in to check the farmhouse. The traps that he'd put in place were untouched, so Frank disarmed them one by one to let himself inside. Even then, he went in there with a pistol drawn, ready for anything. With the resourcefulness she'd shown, he wouldn't have put it past Maya to be there waiting for him, ready to try to kill him.

The building was empty, though. Everything was just as he'd left it, looking rickety and untouched. Frank strode over to a section of floor, pulling up a rug, ripping up the loose floorboards beneath. He paused to disarm the explosive device that he'd set to guard that space, then lifted out a bag.

From it, Frank took out a laptop, burner phones, weapons, money. All the things that he'd thought he might need in a bolt hole like this. These were the resources he had to work with now.

His original plan was in tatters. He couldn't complete the beauty of the full pattern, but he could still make *something* happen. He could improvise and adapt to make something special.

Frank took out a square of card from a drawer, along with a pen. It wasn't much, but he could make it work. One more game, one more chance to make dear Maya do everything that he wanted.

And then, once everything was completed, once she had done everything that he wanted her to do, it would finally be time for this to end. The pattern of this cycle would be complete. Maya would die, with her sister alongside her.

CHAPTER FOUR

Maya stood outside the conference room with Marco, trying not to show any of the worry that she felt that morning as she saw what was waiting for her. It was early, so early that the FBI offices should have been quiet, but there seemed to be more agents around than usual, obviously wanting to know what was going on.

Harris was there in the conference room, of course, but he wasn't the one sitting at the head of the table. That was Director Adams, who was in his fifties, square-jawed with close-cropped hair and spade-like hands. He wore a flag pin in his dark suit and looked particularly severe. Maya had met him once before, when Harris had tried to shut down her small task force.

Agent Swift was on Adams's other side. She was in her late forties, with her blonde hair tied back in a stark bun and understated makeup. She was currently reading through a set of notes that Harris must have supplied. She was the head of the task force that had been hunting the Moonlight Killer for years, and was presumably involved in this proceeding because it had turned out that the unknown man who had kidnapped twelve women and forced Maya to work cases for him was the same notorious serial killer.

There were a couple of other men sitting on one side of the table. To Maya, they looked like they were lawyers, probably up from legal to try to establish if what she'd done had broken any laws.

"You want me to go in there with you?" Marco asked.

Maya shook her head, even though there was nothing she wanted more in that moment than his support.

"I don't want you to get caught up in all of this more than you already are."

"If they fire you, do you seriously think I'll stay?" Marco asked.

"But at least it will be your choice. They'll assume you were just a member of my team. If you go in there and start fighting for me, then you could end up fired, your record could be ruined. Or worse."

Because there was still a chance that this could end up somewhere worse than all of that. The very presence of the lawyers promised it.

"Maya…" Marco began.

Maya shook her head. "I have to be the one to do this. However bad it gets."

Maya walked into the glass-walled conference room. That they were doing this here rather than in Harris's office suggested that Harris wanted the whole department to be able to see what was going on. Or maybe he wanted to emphasize that this had moved beyond any simple departmental level. Maya didn't care. All that mattered to her was getting through this so that she could continue to try to find her sister.

"Agent Grey," Director Adams said. "Take a seat."

He gestured to a spot across from him and Maya sat down, looking from him to Swift to Harris, trying to gauge how this would go. It didn't look good. Harris was obviously unfriendly. Adams looked as though he didn't want to be there and Swift… well, she was essentially impossible to read.

"This is the second time I've been called down to discuss disciplinary action for you, Agent Grey," Adams said.

"And if you remember, sir, the first time I was completely exonerated. Deputy Director Harris has already made it clear that he doesn't like the way I do things."

She didn't care about burning any bridges she had remaining with Harris. He'd already shown that he didn't want her in his department, or even in the FBI, anymore.

"I don't like that you're reckless and that you've put an investigation in danger, withheld evidence, for your own personal reasons," Harris snapped at her.

Maya couldn't help rising to the bait. "*I'm* reckless? The whole reason I have my own task force is because you kept throwing men at raids to try to catch the kidnapper who had taken twelve women without any thought for the danger that would put the hostages in."

"*Had* a task force," Harris corrected her.

Adams brought a hand down on the table sharply. "Enough. I haven't come here to mediate while the two of you argue. Agent Grey, Deputy Director Harris has alleged that you have gone rogue on us. That you're withholding evidence, going off making up your own assignments, refusing to follow orders."

Any one of those might be enough to get Maya thrown out of the bureau. All three? Maya might find herself looking at the inside of a prison cell if she wasn't careful.

"I acted independently, yes," Maya said. "But I had the right to do that as the head of a task force."

"A task force trying to deal with a kidnapper!" Harris snapped. "The moment you found out that the kidnapper was the Moonlight Killer, you should have handed the whole thing over to Agent Swift here."

Agent Swift looked at Maya levelly. "Why *didn't* you inform me that the kidnapper you were chasing was the Moonlight Killer, Agent Grey?"

Maya thought for a moment or two. She knew she couldn't lie, not here, not now.

"Two things. First, while I had things that suggested that the Moonlight Killer might be behind all of this, I never had a definitive piece of evidence to prove that."

"Aside from the fact that he knew which murders were and weren't by the Moonlight Killer," Harris said.

Maya looked over at him. "Hypothetically, someone else might have been able to deduce inconsistencies to work that out. Yes, it was the most likely explanation, but it wasn't something that would stand up in court."

"You weren't interested in court," Harris snapped. "Just in keeping control."

"You said that there were two reasons," Agent Swift said. "What was the second?"

"Operational security. Put simply, my objective was to get the hostages back safely and then to bring the kidnapper to justice. I believed that informing others made it harder to do that."

"How?" Agent Swift asked.

Maya couldn't help looking over at Harris as she said the next part. "I believed that, if I informed others in this office that the kidnapper was the Moonlight Killer, either the killer would react by killing those hostages, or *we* would charge in blindly, disregarding their safety as we tried to catch him."

"What about last night?" Harris asked. There was no give in his tone then. "You went rogue. I'd already given you orders telling you that your task force was being shut down. Hell, I told you to stop the investigation you were working on and come back to DC."

Maya had to bite back her anger. "You told me that I had to be here today. That my task force was being disbanded *today*. I was able to solve my case before that deadline, and to attempt to take down the Moonlight Killer. Because of that, three women are safe and well who would otherwise be dead."

"That's not the order I gave you," Harris said. He just sat there and lied, like it was nothing. "I ordered you to come back at once. I told you that your task force was shut down at once."

"That's a lie," Maya snapped, unable to hold back her anger now.

"Agent Grey, that's enough," Director Adams said. "You do not get to come out and accuse your superior of lying like that."

"Even if that's exactly what he's done?" Maya shot back.

"Do you have any evidence of that?" Director Adams asked.

The worst part was that she didn't. Harris had done it all over the phone. He hadn't put it in writing. There was nothing to say exactly what either of them had or hadn't said.

"No," Maya had to admit.

"Then I have no choice but to take Deputy Director Harris's word about what his orders were. It's possible that there may have been some confusion about that…"

"I was very clear," Harris said, not taking his eyes off Maya. He obviously wasn't going to give her even that much.

Director Adams didn't look happy about it, but he nodded. "Which leads us to a problem, Agent Grey. Yes, you brought in four women. Yes, you've saved others over the past few weeks and brought a number of murderers to justice, but the fact remains that you went against your orders. You went rogue on us, and we *cannot* allow that. What's our legal position?"

He looked over to the lawyers as he said it. They conferred in a whisper for a moment or two before one of them spoke up.

"There are charges on the table relating to dereliction of duty, withholding evidence in an active investigation, and of course, any actions Agent Grey took last night would not be covered. There are potential charges there, too."

Charges? Maya had been worried about that possibility, but she hadn't thought it would come to anything. Were they serious?

"Deputy Director Harris, what's your recommendation on all of this?" Director Adams asked. "Do you want Agent Grey to face charges?"

"I just want her gone," Harris said. "Fired immediately. Her and Detective Spinelli. Why is some Cleveland cop even in my department? If he weren't sleeping with her—"

"Leave Marco out of this," Maya snapped.

"Be quiet," Director Adams said. He put his fingers together as he thought. "Agent Swift, what's your view on this? It's your task force she was withholding evidence from, after all."

This would be the moment that sealed it for Maya. Agent Swift was ambitious and driven. She'd put plenty of time into trying to catch the Moonlight Killer, and she'd made it clear to Maya that she wouldn't tolerate Maya holding back anything from her. Maya had no doubt that the other woman would recommend firing her at least, maybe even try to go along with the lawyers' suggestion of more.

Even as Maya held her breath, though, a knock came on the door of the conference room. It was Marco. He threw open the door and hurried inside without even waiting for the others to invite him in.

"Detective Spinelli, if this is some attempt to make an impassioned plea for clemency, you are going the wrong way about it," Director Adams said.

That was when Maya saw that it wasn't anything like that at all, because she spotted the square of card in Marco's hand, the shape far too familiar. He set the postcard down on the table, the design of a single bunny rabbit with a target on her chest plain to see.

"What's this?" Director Adams demanded.

Maya explained. "It's from the Moonlight Killer. It's how he has been communicating with us throughout this case."

"It just arrived," Marco said. "The internal mail brought it up to your desk, but you were in here."

"If that's from the Moonlight Killer, I want to see it," Agent Swift said. She held out a hand for the card.

Maya wanted to snatch it away from her, to insist on being the one who read it, but before she could get to it Agent Swift had picked up the postcard. The task force head started to read aloud.

"'Dearest Maya, you have disappointed me greatly. I should take your sister from you once and for all for that. But I'm feeling generous. One last game. Lola Marques. One day. Midnight, tonight. You and the detective, if you want his injured body slowing you down. How *are* his wounds doing? Not the rest of the FBI. Any sign that they're helping you, and she dies.'"

Maya swallowed at those words. She was about to be thrown out of the Bureau and the Moonlight Killer was trying to set her another case, giving her another deadline? Yet there was also a wave of relief that hit her in that moment. It meant that her sister was still alive, that there was still a chance to save her.

"This is nonsense," Harris said. "We're the FBI. We've been giving in to his demands for too long."

"If I don't do this," Maya pointed out, "my sister dies. Do you think *anything* will stop me from trying to save her?"

"We could hold you," Harris said. "Keep you in custody to stop you interfering in a case."

Maya narrowed her eyes. "Try."

"This represents our best remaining chance of catching the Moonlight Killer," Agent Swift said. She turned the postcard over in her hands.

"You heard him, no other FBI," Maya said.

"Which is why it *won't* be other FBI," Agent Swift replied. She turned to Director Adams. "You wanted my recommendation, sir? Deputy Director Harris obviously can't handle Agent Grey. So I'd like to transfer her and Detective Spinelli to *my* task force."

"But they ignored orders!" Harris snapped.

Agent Swift gave him a cold look. "All I care about is getting results. If Agent Grey can bring in the Moonlight Killer, then I'll happily put up with her methods. And if not… well, we can revisit this then."

So, Maya would be fine if she succeeded in bringing in the Moonlight Killer, and fired if she didn't? It didn't sound like a great proposition, but right then, it was the only offer on the table.

Assuming it *was* on the table. Maya looked over at Director Adams, knowing that it was his decision that mattered. The seconds seemed to draw out as she waited, unsure which way this would go.

"All right," Adams said. "They're your problem, Swift. Let's just hope that they get some results."

CHAPTER FIVE

Maya read through the files while she and Marco drove over to Chesterford. She found herself wondering as she did so if she should be the one doing the driving, since it was obvious Marco was in pain. He might have been released from the hospital, but it was clear that he wasn't fully recovered yet from the attack that had been designed to keep him from helping Maya with her work.

"Are you sure you're okay to do this?" Maya asked.

"Are you?" Marco countered. "You were shot more recently than I was."

He had a point there, but it wasn't one Maya could let stop her.

"My sister is in danger. I have to help her."

"And *I* have to be there to help *you,*" Marco said, like it was impossible for him to be anywhere else. Maya felt a wave of happiness at that. She hadn't realized just how much she relied on him being by her side until their last case, when the Moonlight Killer had forced her to work it alone.

That was a worry in itself.

"Do you think it will be okay that you're here with me?" Maya asked. Last time, he'd insisted that Marco should stay away from the case or he would kill one of his hostages. The thought that he might hurt Megan because Maya wasn't doing this alone now was almost too much to bear.

"You heard him. He explicitly said that I could help you on this," Marco pointed out. "He thinks I'll slow you down. And there's also the question of how much leverage he has left. When you freed his other hostages, you took away a lot of his power."

Because now, all he had was Megan. Maya wanted to believe that meant that he would keep her safe, that he wouldn't waste her life when she was his only way of getting Maya to do what he wanted, but it was impossible not to worry when a psychopath was involved.

"He has a plan for all of this," Marco said. "He'll want to see it through."

Maya just had to hope that was true. She also felt a lot better now than she had on the last few cases, because she suspected that the Moonlight Killer's ability to surveil her and Marco was drastically curtailed. Not only had she destroyed the phone that he'd bugged, but the fire in the bunker had done a lot to destroy the tools that he'd been using to watch her. He might have others elsewhere, but she doubted that even the Moonlight Killer would be able to replace that kind of setup so easily.

"For now, we need to focus on the case," Marco said. "Tell me what's in the files. I assume it's another murder that was flagged as a Moonlight Killer case?"

"It was," Maya said. She read the file on her laptop. "Although as far as I can see the only reason it was marked as potentially one of his was because the murder took place on the night of the full moon. Lola Marques, twenty-five, killed near the side of a local river. She was tied in place and then stabbed."

"Which is not the Moonlight Killer's MO at all," Marco said.

Maya shook her head. The more murders she'd stripped away as obviously not belonging to the Moonlight Killer, the clearer his methods seemed: he strangled his victims on the night of the full moon using a ligature, then left them where he'd killed them. He didn't take the time to pose them, the way Lola Marques had been. He certainly didn't stab his victims.

"The local police looked for any enemies Lola might have had, but they couldn't find anyone obvious who didn't have an alibi. My guess is that when they couldn't, combined with the full moon, they just grabbed for the first explanation they could find."

"Well, we'll be able to ask the local cops soon enough," Marco said. He nodded to something in the distance.

It took Maya a second or two to realize that it was a town. It seemed to be medium sized, nestled among a few hills, with a river running down the middle of it. Maya could make out the shining forms of a few skyscrapers, but most of the town seemed to be much flatter, almost huddled among the hills as if for shelter.

"That's Chesterford?" Maya asked.

Marco nodded. "We'll be there pretty soon. Where do you want to start with this? Shall we head straight to the crime scene, or talk to the local cops first?"

Maya tried to think. When the two of them only had a day for this, they had to make the right choice here. Ordinarily, she would have gone to the crime scene to get a sense of the way things had happened, but for now, she wanted to know exactly how much progress the local cops had made on the case.

"Let's go talk to the local PD. There are some details in the files, but it feels as though there's a lot that they left out. Maybe they'll be able to tell us something that will help to point us in the right direction."

*

The Chesterford PD was a large concrete and glass building that looked solid and dependable, with a series of patrol cars parked out front. Maya frowned as she saw what looked like a few reporters standing outside the precinct, obviously looking for a story.

Maya found herself wondering what was going on. This couldn't be linked to the Lola Marques murder, because that had been a month ago now. Even the most determined journalist would have given up on the story by now. So what else was going on?

From the moment Maya and Marco pulled up outside the precinct, Maya found cameras pointed her way. As she hurried out of the car, heading for the interior of the precinct, journalists started to yell questions at her.

"Are you with the FBI? Are you here to help with the case?"

"We have no comment at this time," Maya said, trying to keep moving. She had no idea what was going on here, but she wasn't going to risk getting caught up in a media storm when she was so short of time in which to complete her investigation.

She had to push her way through and that hurt, given Maya's injuries. Her stitches felt tight, and she had to be careful as she made her way forward, determined not to tear any of them.

There was a cop blocking the door to keep the reporters out and Maya flashed her badge to get through. She could hear the sound of cameras going off as she did so and winced slightly at the thought of her face being on every news site, with headlines questioning what she was there to do.

Inside, it felt as though everything was moving far faster than a precinct in a town like this normally would have been. Maya saw cops running around, saw a couple obviously there to make sure that no reporters got through, saw the nerves on officers' faces. That was worrying. Even outside a major city, what could be big enough to make cops look that worried?

Maya looked at Marco. "What do you think is going on?"

She saw Marco shrug. "It's hard to say. Let's find out."

He and Maya walked over to a man who appeared to be a detective, in his forties, wearing slacks and a brown jacket over an underarm holster. His badge was on a chain around his neck. His hair was dark but with a few flecks of gray in it, and his blue eyes looked at Maya with a note of suspicion.

"I don't know you. If you're a reporter, we've already said everything we're going to say."

Maya held up her badge. She saw the detective stare at it with a note of surprise.

"You're here already?"

That made Maya frown, not understanding. "What do you mean 'already'? Didn't you get a call from our boss to say that we were coming?"

She'd assumed that Agent Swift would call ahead, but maybe the task force head had been busy focusing on other things.

"*We're* the ones who put in a call, less than an hour ago. You're not here about the murder we had last night?"

Maya didn't know anything about any murder the previous evening, although that would account for the sudden increase in activity around the precinct compared to what she might have expected. She wasn't there for whatever had happened last night, though; she'd been sent by the Moonlight Killer to look into only one case.

"I'm Agent Grey, this is Detective Spinelli," Maya said.

"I'm Detective Tanner. You're really not here because of Helene Gretting?"

"We're here because of the Lola Marques murder."

"Lola Marques?" That got another look of surprise from the detective. "But… those two cases are linked."

That was enough to make Maya stop short. She felt as though she'd been dropped into the middle of this without enough information. She stood there, taking a breath, forcing herself to slow down.

"Why don't you explain what's happening?" she suggested to Detective Tanner. She didn't like walking into all of this only to find something unexpected going on.

Detective Tanner nodded. "We had a tip last night. One of our officers, Sorenson, went to investigate. He found… well, he found a body, posed exactly the way Lola Marques had been, stabbed the same way. It *has* to be the same killer."

Maya looked over at Marco, who nodded. It seemed that they'd stumbled into the investigation for another murder by the same man. That left Maya wondering if the Moonlight Killer had known that it was going to happen. If he'd sent her now because he'd known that this killer would strike again. How far ahead of her was he on all of this?

"There's just one thing," Detective Tanner said. "If you're here hunting the Moonlight Killer, I'm sorry, but it looks like you might be in the wrong place. It wasn't a full moon last night, we're still a couple of nights away from it."

"And the killer stabbed the victims, as well as posing them, which the Moonlight Killer doesn't do," Maya said.

Detective Tanner stared at her, looking worried. "Does that mean that you're not here to help after all?"

"We are," Maya assured him. "We're investigating this murder, *these* murders, in relation to another investigation. We need to get answers on this as much as you do, Detective."

More than he did, because it wasn't *his* sister's life in the balance if Maya didn't find answers soon.

Detective Tanner looked relieved by that, obviously happy that his department didn't have to take the lead on this anymore.

"What do you need from us?" Tanner asked. "Where do you want to start?"

Maya thought for a moment. The shape of this case had changed now that there were two murders instead of one, but that didn't change the way she wanted to investigate it.

"We'll need to talk to Officer Sorenson. We'll also need to take a look at last night's crime scene. Maybe there's something there we can go on."

Detective Tanner nodded. "I'll give you the address and have him meet you there. I just hope you're able to make some progress with this, Agent Grey. One murder like this is horrifying enough, but two… there's a lot of pressure on me to resolve this."

Not as much as there was on Maya. She was already hurrying toward the door. She needed to find answers, and there was hardly any time to do it.

CHAPTER SIX

For Maya, it was all too easy to imagine someone being able to commit murder in the park without being spotted.

Even with the whole area around the murder scene closed off, even with reporters crowded on the edge of the police tape, even with forensic techs still going over the scene on their hands and knees, it was still easy to see how lonely this place would be at night.

There were stands of trees that would obscure any view from the surrounding roads, while the murder had taken place deep enough into the park that, even if any screams carried out to the rest of Chesterford, the killer could have been long gone by the time anyone arrived to help.

The crime scene wasn't far from an old bandstand, on a patch of open ground a little way in front of it, the morning sun beaming down on it without a hint of shade from the surrounding trees.

"What do you think of this as a kill spot?" Maya asked Marco.

She saw him look around, obviously sizing it up.

"There are good escape routes and it's private, but…"

"But?" Maya asked.

"Why was the kill there, rather than in the bandstand or in one of the groups of trees? If the killer was looking for somewhere private where he wouldn't be spotted, why do it in the most open part of the park?"

"Maybe that's just where Helene Gretting was?" Maya suggested. The Moonlight Killer always stalked his victims, striking at some point in their everyday lives under the moonlight. He killed them where he found them, and then left them where he found them. Was it possible that this killer was the same?

As Maya got closer to the crime scene, though, she knew that she was wrong. There was nothing accidental about the location, because this wasn't a killer who just abandoned his victims.

Helene Gretting's body had been taken away by the coroner, but there was still a framework there that had obviously been designed to hold her in place. It was made from a combination of wood and metal, looking solid enough that Maya couldn't imagine it being constructed quickly.

“He either built this quietly here or, more likely, he built it somewhere else and brought it with him,” Maya said. “Either way, it must have taken a lot of effort.”

“Which means a lot of planning,” Marco said. “This isn’t some wild killer just lashing out at random.”

In a way, that was a good thing. It suggested a killer who had a deliberate pattern and a purpose, one that might be unraveled to lead back to him. Maya realized with a sudden rush of horror just how easily the Moonlight Killer could have sent her after a different kind of murderer this time, one who couldn’t be caught within the timeframe he’d allotted.

Previously, he’d played fair, according to the rules of his own game, but what if this *wasn’t* about the game anymore? What if this was just a way to force Maya to fail? What if he planned on killing her sister regardless of what happened? It was a terrifying thought.

“What if there’s no way to solve this in time?” Maya asked, voicing her fears.

Marco put a reassuring hand on her shoulder. “We’ll find a way, Maya.”

“But what if he’s deliberately picked something that can’t be solved?”

Marco shook his head. “Then there would be no reason for him to do all of this. He would have just killed Megan and left. You know that if he’s doing all of this, it’s because he can’t just give up on whatever he’s doing.”

Maya knew that. She’d even thought it, back in DC. She still couldn’t shake the feeling, though, that this case might be different, that the Moonlight Killer might not *want* her to succeed.

For now, though, Maya had to focus on the case. She had to put aside her fears and do everything she could to find answers in this case. Once she *had* those answers, she was worried that the Moonlight Killer might try to find a way to double-cross her, but at that point, Maya would simply have to do everything she could to make sure her sister came out of this safe.

A police officer came up to them. To Maya, he looked almost too young to be on the force, with short, sandy hair and boyish features. Probably he just looked younger than he was, but Maya couldn’t imagine that he’d been a part of the Chesterford PD for long.

“Are you the FBI?” he asked.

Maya showed her badge. “I’m Agent Grey, and this is Detective Spinelli.”

"I'm Bret Sorenson."

This was the officer who had found the body? Maya could only imagine how that would affect him, if he really was as new to the department as he looked. It was hard for Maya to put herself into that mindset, because she'd worked on so many murder cases now, tracked down so many killers. She'd seen the aftermath of so much death and it still affected her, but not quite as sharply as it had the first time. Experience had changed that for her.

"Officer Sorenson, you're the one who found Helene Gretting?"

"That's right, ma'am. I only joined the force last month. It was one of my first times out on patrol alone."

Maya was less than a decade older than him, but right then, it felt like a lifetime.

"Can you tell us what happened?" Maya asked.

The cop shrugged. "There isn't much I can say. I got a call through from control while I was working my beat, just over that way." He nodded back in the direction of some expensive-looking properties just visible beyond the fringes of the park.

Maya briefly wondered if this spot would be visible from there. Was there a chance that this choice of murder site was specifically to allow it to be seen, either by those who lived there or by the killer, watching from a vantage point? She didn't think the former was likely, especially in the dark, but the latter was just about possible. Maybe this killer liked to watch the reaction to his work?

"We'll need to get someone to check security footage for the houses over that way, to see if anyone was lurking, watching in the direction of the park," Maya said.

"It's a long shot," Marco pointed out.

"I know, but we have to try everything."

Maya knew that she and Marco couldn't spend their time pursuing that potential lead, but they also couldn't allow it to go uninvestigated. Maya focused on Officer Sorenson again.

"There was a tip for the Lola Marques murder as well, wasn't there?" Maya said, remembering that from the file.

"I think so," Sorenson said. "I didn't know that until backup showed up and they told me. I didn't even know all the details of the first murder."

Because he was so new he hadn't even been on the force when Lola Marques had been killed.

"Let's backtrack," Maya said. "You got the tip, you came to the park. What then? What did you see?"

"At first, I didn't think there was anyone there," Sorenson said. "Then I thought it must just be some drunk or something, I was trying to move them on. Then, as I got closer…"

Maya could hear the pain in his voice. Thankfully, it wasn't the moment when he'd discovered the body that she needed him to focus on.

"Did you see anyone else? Or any sign that someone might have still been there?"

Officer Sorenson shook his head. "I didn't see anything other than… this."

He gestured to the construction that had been there, presumably to hold the body in the pose that the killer had wanted.

Maya wondered if he hadn't seen anything because there was nothing to see, or because the distraction of the body had made it impossible to look anywhere else. Would the killer have been there, watching?

"Have the forensics team come up with anything so far?" Maya asked.

Sorenson shook his head. "Nothing. The killer was careful."

Which fit with the idea that he'd planned all of this carefully. Maya went over to the wood and metal structure that the killer had used to display his victim. It had a kind of tripod base, then a solid metal pole with brackets that were probably there to allow the victim to be tied in place more easily. An armlike extension jutted out from it, presumably to force the victim into the posture he wanted. It was obviously custom built, presumably by the killer, although they would need to be sure.

"We'll need to get local PD to check with local wood and metal workers, just in case the killer got someone else to build this for him," Maya said.

Marco nodded. "What do you think all of this is about?"

"I'm not sure yet," Maya admitted. She gestured to the structure. "This seems to be about display. All of it does. The anonymous tips to the police, the deliberate posing of the bodies, the effort this killer is taking to make sure the scene is exactly the way he wants. It all suggests a killer who wants his work to be seen. He wants the attention that comes from this."

"But then, why not kill somewhere more people would see it?" Marco asked. "Why not just walk up and stab someone in the street? If he planned it carefully, he could do it without cameras tracking him."

"Because this means something to him," Maya said. "This is how he wants to display his victims. He wants to create this particular scene, either because it's an effect he wants to create or because it's something to do with the victims. I'm more interested in the question of why Lola Marques was here at that time for him to kill. Was this some kind of regular route for her? Through a deserted park at night?"

It didn't seem that likely to her. Certainly, it wasn't a route she could imagine most women taking, when there were well-lit streets around the park that they might use instead. Did that mean that the killer had actually attacked Lola Marques somewhere else, then brought her here to display her? If so, why here?

"You're right," Marco said. "We need to find out if there's another crime scene somewhere else, somewhere that might have more evidence than this display site."

"We also need to find out if there are any links between the victims," Maya said. "With the effort the killer has put in here, and how much planning was involved, is it really plausible that he would pick his victims at random?"

"Maybe, if the kill and the display are the important parts for him," Marco said, "but it's much more likely that there's a connection somewhere. It's clearly not something obvious, though, or the local cops would have found it already."

That was true. It might only have been a few hours since the murder, but the Chesterford PD would have thrown all the resources they had at it in those hours. If there were anything obvious to find, Maya had to believe that they would have found it.

She needed to find a way to go deeper, to learn what she could about the life of Helene Gretting and maybe gain access to her online footprint. The quickest way to do that would be to talk to her family.

Maya just had to hope that there would be something there that would provide a connection. She needed something that would give her a way forward in this case, both before this killer had a chance to strike again and before the Moonlight Killer lost patience and Megan died.

CHAPTER SEVEN

"Are you okay?"

Marco could see Maya's tension as the two of them drove up to the house belonging to Helene Gretting's sister.

"It's just with this being her sister. I know what she's going through."

Marco shook his head. "You don't, though, Maya. Megan isn't dead. You're going to save her."

He had to remind her of that, even if the situation was dangerous, even if the odds weren't in their favor on all of this. They were going to do everything they could to both get Megan back and take the Moonlight Killer down.

Maya nodded. "But I can still imagine how bad it might be. The idea of losing a sister like that…"

Marco could understand that, but he knew he needed to get her to focus. "It's good that you have sympathy for her, Maya, but you know that the best thing you can do for her, and for Megan, is to get the answers you need to catch this killer."

It worried him a little that he needed to remind Maya of that, because normally, she was utterly focused and good at her job. If anything, Marco occasionally had to hold her back. He *didn't* normally have to remind her that she could do her job, that she *should* do her job, rather than getting lost in the pity that she felt for the dead.

"I'm glad you're here for this," Maya said. Her hand closed over his. It was only brief, but Marco found himself focusing on that moment of connection.

"I'm glad I am too," Marco replied. They pulled up outside the small suburban house that belonged to Helene's sister. "Now, before we go in, is there anything in the files that I need to know?"

He'd left it to Maya to skim them while he drove over. She was good at absorbing large quantities of information, finding unusual connections.

"The first thing is that this is also Helene Gretting's address," Maya said.

"She lived with her sister?" Marco replied.

"It looks that way. The local cops have been here to notify the sister, Isobel, of what's happened, and they got a basic statement from her, but I want to hear the details for myself."

"Have any details come through from the crime scene?" Marco asked. The more evidence they had going into this, the better chance they had of making meaningful connections.

"There are some preliminary notes from the coroner and forensics," Maya said. "The coroner says that the blood spatter at the scene is consistent with Helene Gretting being killed there, but there are also drag marks nearby."

"Meaning that the killer subdued her somewhere else and then moved her into position to kill her?"

"Exactly."

Marco tried to imagine the effort that must have taken, and the additional risk. Ambushing and killing someone created enough problems when it came to potentially leaving evidence behind, but trying to subdue someone and then take them to a secondary location?

"If we can work out where, then there's a chance that someone heard or saw the initial abduction," Marco said. "With something like that, she would have been trying to fight or call out for help."

"Unless the killer overwhelmed her very quickly," Maya said. "Or unless she thought that cooperating was her best chance to survive. But yes, we should try to identify where she was taken from. Maybe her sister will be able to help us with that."

That seemed to be their cue to head over to the house. The door opened as they walked up, revealing a woman in her twenties, a little shorter than Maya, slender and dark haired, wearing jeans and a dark sweater. To Marco, she looked as though she'd been crying. This had to be Isobel Gretting.

"If you're more reporters—"

"We're with the FBI, Ms. Gretting," Maya said, holding up her badge. "I'm Agent Grey and this is my partner, Marco Spinelli. We were hoping that we could talk to you. May we come in?"

"I… yes, I guess so. Why is the FBI involved in this?"

Marco took that, knowing that they couldn't explain any of the reasons to do with the Moonlight Killer.

"We think there's a link to an earlier case," Marco said.

"The Lola Marques one? That's what all the reporters were saying."

"Why don't we go inside so that we can talk about it?" Marco suggested.

Isobel nodded and stepped back out of the way, showing them into a house that was tastefully if rather plainly decorated, with only a few pictures on the walls, mostly showing Isobel and a woman who looked a lot like her. It occurred to Marco that, because he hadn't been the one to look through the files, he didn't know for sure if it was Helene Gretting.

To Marco, the house seemed a little cluttered, as if there were two sets of everything vying for space everywhere he looked. There was an almost overflowing shoe rack by the door, a stack of coats set one atop another on the banister of the stairs, even competing stacks of books as Isobel showed them into a small living room, gesturing for Marco and Maya to take a seat on a couch.

"Sorry about the mess," Isobel said, curling up in an armchair, hugging her knees tightly as if to comfort herself. "It was just, with Helene living here with me, she brought all her stuff and..."

She choked up for a moment. Marco had seen that kind of reaction before, where people tried briefly to pretend that things were normal while they were grieving, only to realize that it wasn't possible. Grief always found a way to push through, however hard people tried.

"We're very sorry for your loss," Maya said. Marco could hear the sympathy in her voice. "We also want to try to catch the person who did this."

"Good," Isobel said, looking suddenly determined.

"Isobel," Maya said, "Helene was found in a park in the Three Hills district. Was that somewhere she normally went?"

"She had a job in one of the bars there in the evening," Isobel said.

"And would she have walked back through the park?"

Isobel shook her head sharply. "She was always complaining that some of the customers could be creeps, that she didn't want to be alone with them. No, she always just walked back to her car and drove home."

Marco made a mental note to check with the Chesterford PD whether they'd found Helene's car.

"Were there any customers she was particularly worried by?" Marco asked. "Did she ever mention any names?"

Both of the victims had been young women. Was it possible that this was simply down to some guy they'd both rejected? Some guy who had decided to take revenge in the most brutal way possible?

Isobel shook her head. "She just talked about them in general terms. It was always just some guy, you know?"

Marco nodded. Maya seemed to have an idea, though.

"You said before that there's a lot of your sister's stuff here. Does that include a computer or a phone? One that you know the password for?"

Isobel nodded. "Hold on. I think her tablet is here somewhere."

She dug around in one of the piles of books, coming up with a computer tablet, which she unlocked before passing it to Maya.

"If it's all right, I want to use this to look through Helene's social media and emails to try to find if there's anyone who might have threatened her."

"All right," Isobel said. "You can take it with you, if you need it."

"Thank you." Maya started to look through it quickly, obviously searching for anything that stood out enough that she would need to follow it up with Isobel right away. While she did that, Marco tried to learn more about Helene from her sister, trying to find anything that might form a link between the two murders.

He started with the most obvious question. "Did your sister know Lola Marques?"

Isobel shook her head. "I'm sorry, I think the first time I ever heard that name was in the news, and it wasn't like Helene reacted when she was killed, or anything."

Which suggested the two of them didn't know one another. Any connection between them would have to come another way.

"Tell me more about your sister," Marco said, while Maya continued to look through Helene Gretting's online presence. "You said she worked at a bar, but what else did she do? How did she spend her time? Where did she go?"

"She was taking a couple of college courses," Isobel said. "The bar work and living here with me were all about just trying to keep going with college. She'd go off to the library a lot, go out running, go out with her friends. I'm sorry, I'm not sure what I can tell you."

"That's fine," Marco assured her. "I'm just trying to get more of a picture of Helene's life."

That way if any parts of it lined up with Lola Marques's life, they would be more likely to make the connection.

"Was your sister seeing anyone?" Marco asked.

"No, I don't think so."

"Had she broken up with anyone recently? Anyone who might still be angry with her about it?"

"You think this was over a *breakup*?"

"We don't know what this was about yet," Maya supplied, still working on Helene's tablet. "We need to look at every possibility. *Had* she broken up with anyone recently?"

"No, she was focused on her studies. Oh, there were guys, but there was never anything serious, and not recently."

"And can you think of anyone at all who might have wanted to hurt your sister?" Marco asked. "Had she argued with anyone recently? Had anyone started behaving strangely around her?"

"No," Isobel said, shaking her head. "Look, I'm sorry. I really don't know anything. Shouldn't you be out there, looking for whoever did this?"

It was obvious that she didn't want them there, intruding on her grief. Marco looked over to Maya, who nodded.

"I think we have everything we need for now," she said. "But we'll need to take the tablet with us as evidence. Is that all right?"

"Yes, that's fine," Isobel said. She stood up, an obvious signal that it was time for Marco and Maya to leave.

The two of them headed out to the car together.

"Is there anything on her social media?" Marco asked.

"Nothing obvious," Maya replied. "No threats or arguments that might have prompted someone to kill her, but maybe there will be something here that links to Lola Marques once we talk to her family too."

"That's where we're heading next?"

Maya nodded. Marco hoped they would be able to find something there that would provide them with a connection between the two victims. Without that, they had no idea why the killer was doing this, and when, or if, he would strike next.

CHAPTER EIGHT

"This is the place," Maya said.

Maya hoped, as they pulled up in front of the Marques family home, that this would be the place where she and Marco would find something that would get them deeper into the investigation. Without it, she wasn't sure where to look next.

The house was a large family home, not the place where Lola had lived, but her parents' home. Maya had called ahead, so she knew that they would be there to meet her and Marco, but even so, she found herself worrying about whether the two of them would be able to get anything useful here when Isobel Gretting hadn't been able to tell them much.

Still, they had to try. She and Marco left the car, heading up a short driveway with an SUV parked on it to the front door. Almost as soon as Maya rang the bell, it was answered by a woman in her fifties, short and blonde-haired, wearing a floral print dress.

"Hello, I'm Agent Grey with the FBI, this is Detective Spinelli."

"Ellen Marques, come in."

She led the way into the house. It should have seemed warm and inviting, painted as it was in neutral tones and with family portraits up around the walls, but there was a sense in there of something wrong, of a tension that wouldn't leave. It took Maya a moment to realize that tension was in Ellen Marques's every movement, and in the strain that lay under the smile on her face.

After a murder, that was easy for Maya to understand. She only hoped that she and Marco bringing the killer to justice would do something to alleviate it.

They went through into a modern, open-plan kitchen, sitting at a table there, where a window gave a view out onto the house's yard. A tall, dark-haired Latino man was there, hacking at the shrubbery in the garden as if it had done something to anger him personally.

"That's my husband, Rodrigo. He isn't taking all of this very well," Ellen said, moving to join them at the kitchen table. "Can you tell me if there has been any progress on my daughter's case?"

"We're reinvestigating it," Maya said. "Trying to go through everything to see if we can find any fresh angles."

"But do you think you'll be able to catch anyone?" Ellen asked.

"We hope so," Maya said. "Can you tell us about your daughter? What did she do? Who were her friends? That kind of thing."

Maya saw Lola's mother think for a few seconds.

"Lola used to work at a gallery in town. She always said that she wanted to be an artist when she was growing up, but then when she got into her twenties, she decided that she was better at selling paintings than painting them. I always thought her work was so good, though. I used to put it up around the house everywhere."

Maya hadn't noticed any paintings on the way in, though, only photographs.

"Where is that work now?" she asked.

Ellen shook her head. "Rodrigo put it in the garage. He says he can't stand to look at it, because it hurts like losing her all over again every time." A flash of pain crossed her face then. "I have to go in there and stare at them sometimes. He doesn't get that it's not just him hurting."

It was difficult, even now, walking in on people's grief. Until recently, Maya hadn't had to deal with it this way, because she'd been working cases that had been cold for a long time, cases where the loss and the pain weren't as raw or as immediate.

"What about Lola's friends?" Maya asked, both to try to move Ellen away from her pain and to try to learn anything she could that might be relevant to the case. "Did she have any disagreements with them in the days leading up to her death? Or have any of them said anything to you about things seeming different with her, like something might have been going on that might have been dangerous?"

"No, nothing like that," Ellen said. "The police asked us that, and we told them that our girl would never be involved in anything that might have done *this* to her."

"We're only asking in case you have remembered anything that didn't occur to you at the time," Marco said in a soothing tone. "Maybe your daughter was involved in a big project at work?"

"Lola didn't mention anything like that. She used to get so excited when a new artist was going to have a show there. She would have said something."

"Did she have any conflicts at work with anyone?" Maya asked. "Maybe a difficult artist, or one of the clients there?"

"No, I'm sorry. There's never been anything like that. My daughter loved her job."

Meaning that the cause of her death was unlikely to be there, or at least that Lola Marques hadn't told her family about it if it was. Maya knew that she needed to keep going, though. Every aspect of Lola's life she asked about was one more where there was a chance of a connection to Helene Gretting.

Maya decided to ask that outright. "Did Lola ever mention someone named Helene Gretting? She worked in a bar up in the Three Hills district."

Ellen thought for a moment. "I don't recall her ever using the name."

Maya was about to try to make certain of that when Rodrigo Marques came in from the yard, not looking happy at all.

"Are they still here?" he demanded.

Maya saw Ellen wince.

"Rodrigo, they need to ask their questions."

"What questions? The same ones the police asked a month ago? Can we think of anyone who would want to kill our daughter? Do we know why this has happened? Like *we're* the detectives, not them?"

Maya knew that this was the kind of anger that came from grief, so she did her best to stay calm in the face of it, rather than rising to it the way she might have under other circumstances.

"Mr. Marques, we're just trying to get as complete a picture as possible for our new investigation."

"The police have *had* a 'complete picture' for a month!" Rodrigo said, gesturing sharply. Maya's gaze was on the shears that he still had in his hand. She didn't think he was about to start using them as a weapon, but it would be far too easy for him to lash out with them by accident.

"We're just looking for anything that you might have thought of since then," Marco said. "Anything that might have slipped your mind at the time, but which you now think might be relevant."

"Slipped my mind? You think I can forget *anything* about all this when my daughter is dead? Besides, I already *told* the cops who did this."

That took Maya a little by surprise. "And who was that, Mr. Marques?"

She could see the frustration on Rodrigo's face. He obviously hated having to go through all of this again, but now that he'd said something like that, Maya had to know what he meant. "We all know it's that good-for-nothing ex-boyfriend of hers. But no, the police had to let him go. He got himself a fancy lawyer or something, got himself released."

That was something they needed to check. If the police had already dismissed the boyfriend as a suspect, it probably wasn't worth spending too much time on him, but in the absence of other leads, it was probably worth at least looking into him briefly.

"Tell me about this boyfriend," Maya said.

"*Ex*-boyfriend. Sammy Christopher. He used to roll up here in some sixty-seven Firebird he thought was going to impress people. Obsessed with it. Me, it just made me wonder where a kid with no steady job got the money."

"What happened with him and Lola?" Maya asked.

Ellen answered. "He was no good for her. He didn't treat her right. And then it was more than that. The first time he laid a hand on her, she walked out on him, didn't look back."

That caught Maya's interest even further. An ex-boyfriend the victim's parents thought might be a suspect was one thing. An abusive ex-boyfriend was potentially something more.

"Do you know where he went?" Maya asked.

Rodrigo's eyes narrowed. "He skipped town the moment the cops let him go. Probably realized what I would do if I ever got my hands on him."

A suspect who had left town? Again, it made him more interesting. Certainly interesting enough to look into.

"Thank you," Maya said, with a gesture to Marco that they should leave. "You've both been very helpful."

The two of them headed back out to the car. There, Maya looked through the files to find any reference to Sammy Christopher. It turned out that the police had questioned him but quickly let him go because his lawyer had pointed out their lack of physical evidence, their lack of witnesses, their lack of… well, anything tying him to the murder.

That was also a potential problem for Maya. How much time could she and Marco put into questioning a suspect who had already been cleared? She was determined to look a little closer at him, though.

A quick search showed that he had a police record, with several arrests for what appeared to be small cons and minor assaults. None of it seemed to have stuck to him, though, with no convictions, nothing that even seemed to have gotten as far as court.

Maya looked for him on social media and quickly found an old account with a picture of a good-looking young man in his twenties, dark-haired and with chiseled features, athletic and dressed in expensive clothes while trying to look tough. There were a *lot* of pictures of him with his car. Exactly the kind of bad-boy image Maya could imagine someone falling for until they realized that it wasn't just an image.

The strange thing was that there were no new updates, no sign that Sammy Christopher even still existed. It was like he'd vanished into thin air.

"If he's moved to a different town, maybe changed his name to lie low, then it could be hard to find him," Maya said. She tried the DMV. There was no one under Sammy's name living locally. "It would be like looking for a needle in a haystack."

"So we pick a needle that's easier to spot," Marco said. He pointed at one of the pictures of Sammy's car. "If he really does love his car as much as Rodrigo thinks, then my guess is that he won't have just gotten rid of it. And if he did, at least we should be able to talk to whoever he sold it to and find him that way."

He had a point. Maya ran the car through the DMV, rather than the name, and quickly came up with a hit: Samuel C. Lawrentine. When she looked *that* name up on social media, Maya wasn't surprised to find the same chiseled features as before staring back at her, although with a much more clean-cut image.

Maya found herself wondering if Sammy Christopher had ever really existed, or if maybe this was the real version of him. Either way, the combination of the deception, the brushes with the cops, and the alleged abuse made him a much better suspect than he'd seemed just minutes before.

Maya wanted to talk to Samuel Lawrentine, even if it meant a trip to the next town.

CHAPTER NINE

Maya spent most of the thirty-minute drive over to the town of Hartby feeling the seconds ticking away, knowing that this was a big commitment of time in a case where they only had around a day and a half left.

They had to do it, though. When they had a suspect who had skipped town and changed his name, that raised too many flags to ignore. At least they had an address for this new version of him, in an apartment building near the center of the small town, a building that looked surprisingly expensive to Maya's eyes.

She looked around for the Firebird in front of the building. There was no sign of it there and that worried her a little. Was he just not at home, or had Samuel moved on again?

They headed into the building, taking the stairs up to the second floor, where Samuel's apartment was.

"How do you want to approach this?" Marco asked as they walked up to the door. "Do we treat him more like a potential witness who can give us information, or do we go in harder with him, try to put pressure on him from the start?"

It was a good question. They could try to be harder with Samuel, and hope that the shock of the FBI showing up at his door would get him to let something slip, but there was a risk that he would simply clam up and refuse to say anything. On the other hand, if they went too softly with him, there was a risk that it would just give him the time he needed to work out what was going on and to get his story straight. With so little time to conduct the investigation, Maya's initial instinct was to push hard for answers, but she overrode that instinct.

"We'll start softly. The local PD let him go, after all. And looking at his record, he'll lawyer up at the first sign of trouble. If he doesn't have good answers for us, then we'll try to put a bit more pressure on."

"Okay," Marco said. "Although his record probably also means he isn't going to say much if he doesn't feel he has to."

"At that point, we'll make sure that he feels he has to."

Maya stepped up to knock on the door to the apartment, then moved off to the side slightly. She'd been attacked too many times now coming to talk to suspects not to be at least a little cautious.

The door opened after a few moments, revealing a young man in sweatpants and a T-shirt. The only problem was that this wasn't Samuel. This young man was shorter, with a round face and red hair. He stared up at Maya through the lenses of thick glasses.

"Yes?"

Maya held up her badge. "I'm Agent Grey, with the FBI. Is Samuel Lawrentine here?"

"You want to talk to Samuel?" The information seemed to be taking a moment or two to sink in with this young man, but even so, Maya felt a note of relief. His recognition at the use of Samuel's name said that they had the right place.

"That's right. Who are you, please?"

"I'm Joey, Samuel's roommate. He needed someone to help with the rent and…" Maya could hear the nerves in his voice.

"Is Samuel here?" Marco asked, obviously trying to get the young man to focus. Maybe he just didn't want to risk giving Samuel a chance to run.

That thought made Maya look past Joey, into a gray-painted apartment with views out over the rest of the town. She was watching out for any sign of someone trying to run out to a fire escape. She couldn't hear anything there beyond Joey, though.

"He's not here," Joey said. "He's at work."

"Do you know where he works?" Maya asked.

"Sure, he's down at Verison-Smythe." Joey picked up a piece of mail as he said it, the headed notepaper of what appeared to be a consultancy firm visible at the top. Maya made a quick note of the address.

A part of Maya wanted to rush off there to question Samuel, but something made her pause. She had a potential source of new information right in front of her, and she was determined to make the most of that opportunity.

"Joey, can you tell me about Samuel?" she asked. "What's he like?"

"He's… well, he's a smart, funny guy, I guess," Joey said. He didn't sound entirely certain.

"You guess?"

"Well…" There was another moment of hesitation from Samuel's roommate. "Look, he's good at getting people to do what he wants, but he's behind on the rent and he's kind of an asshole about some things. Like, he never seems to pay for anything unless someone's watching, and he's always boasting about the ways he manipulates people."

Including Joey, Maya suspected. Because she guessed that Samuel had no intention of ever paying his share of the rent. The more she heard about him, the more certain she felt that this was some petty con man.

Did that give him a motive to kill the two victims? Was it possible that Lola Marques had worked out some scheme of his and he'd killed her for it?

Maya didn't know, but she knew where to find him now to ask.

*

To Maya, the offices where Samuel currently worked seemed tastefully and elegantly designed not to look like offices at all. More like some kind of expensive country club on the edge of town where people just happened to do business. As she and Marco walked in, a receptionist moved to intercept them, flashing a professional smile. She was probably more expensively dressed than Maya was, with perfect makeup and not a single dark hair out of place.

"Can I help you?" Something about her tone tried to suggest that it was almost impossible for her to imagine a way in which she could help two people who looked like Maya and Marco.

"FBI," Maya said. She caught the suddenly worried look on the receptionist's face. "We're not here for anything to do with the company, but we *do* need to talk to one of the employees here."

"Can't it wait?" the receptionist asked. Clearly, the idea of the FBI doing anything to disrupt the running of the business was anathema to her. She'd clearly been told that a part of her job was to make sure that the business environment remained serene, without the wrong kind of people getting in.

"No," Maya said. "It can't. We need to talk to Samuel Lawrentine urgently."

They didn't have any time to waste when the Moonlight Killer had given them such a short deadline, and when Megan's life continued to hang in the balance. *Especially* not with a suspect who had already left town and changed his name once.

The receptionist looked as though she might argue about it, but obviously realized just how much trouble that might cause.

"I can call him down here if you want," the receptionist said.

Maya shook her head. She didn't want to give Samuel that kind of advance warning. She didn't want to spend half an hour waiting here while Samuel slipped out of another entrance and got away. If he was the killer, or even just the con man he appeared to be, there was a good chance that he wouldn't wait around for the FBI to catch up to him.

"We'll go to him. Where can we find him?"

The receptionist seemed to consider for another couple of seconds before she gave in. "Fourth floor."

Maya made her way over to an elevator with Marco, heading up to the fourth floor. The moment the elevator doors opened, Maya started to wonder if they were still in the same office building. This wasn't the kind of expensive elegance that had been in the reception area, but instead was just a large maze of cubicles, figures in them working away on computers, talking loudly into phones, and occasionally arguing with one another.

A man in his forties came up to them. He was wearing slacks, a white shirt with the sleeves rolled up, and red suspenders. He had a bushy brown beard with a single white streak running through it.

"You're not supposed to be up here."

Maya held her badge out in front of herself to avoid getting into a long argument about it.

"FBI. We're looking for Samuel Lawrentine."

Even as she said it, Maya caught sudden movement out of the corner of her eye. She saw a man pop up from one of the cubicles and then start to run. It took her only a fraction of a second to recognize Samuel from his photographs.

"Samuel! Stop right there!"

He kept running, and Maya set off in pursuit. She glanced around at Marco, then nodded to the maze of cubicles.

"Split up!" Maya called out, knowing that in a place like this, their best chance lay in trying to come at their suspect from both sides.

She pushed her way forward past a couple of the people who worked there, trying to keep moving, trying not to let the close press of the cubicles slow her down too much. Many of the cubicle dividers were higher than Maya's head, so that it was impossible to get a clear view out over the whole of the office, or to see which way Samuel had gone.

All Maya could do was to take the twists and turns of it nearly at random, trying to keep moving in the general direction that Samuel had been going in, trying to ignore the fact that she was advancing almost blind on someone who might have murdered two women.

Maya didn't even know where Marco was anymore. He was somewhere in the maze of cubicles, and his height meant that there were occasional brief glimpses of him in more open sections of the office, but for the most part he was invisible. There were only the gray cubicle walls around Maya, punctuated by occasional notices put there by the firm's management.

Ahead, Maya could see a set of doors leading to a stairwell. The doors were just swinging closed and that was all the incentive Maya needed to run for them. She hurried through them, looking up, then down, trying to catch a glimpse of her suspect. Maya thought she heard the sound of running feet below and that was all she needed to head after Samuel again, taking the stairs as fast as she could.

Maya got out her phone, calling Marco as she ran.

"He's heading for the ground floor."

Maya shoved the phone back into her jacket pocket, continuing to run. She reached ground level and saw Samuel ahead, just exiting the building. Maya sprinted after him, determined to close the gap. She ran out into the open air, into the grassy surrounds of the company.

Samuel was there, heading for a corner of the business's parking lot. Maya could see his car there waiting for him. If he got to it, he could be away and gone. They might never catch up to him again.

"You're not getting away that easily," Maya said as she ran forward, determined to beat him to the car. Even as she said it, though, she felt the pain in her side from pushing too hard with an injury. Maya did her best to ignore it, but the pain wouldn't let her have the burst of speed she was looking for, wouldn't let her catch up.

Samuel was at the car now, getting in it. They were going to lose him.

That was when Maya saw Marco pulling their car forward, moving to block Samuel's parking space. He'd obviously gone straight for the car, knowing that he couldn't help keep up with Samuel in a foot race, given his own injuries. It was good thinking, and Maya wished that she'd come up with it herself because of the pain she was now in. Had she blown one of her stitches?

Maya ignored that pain and made her way over to the spot where Samuel had parked his Firebird. She took out her gun, leveling it at him through the windshield.

"Show me your hands, Samuel! Get out of the car slowly. You're under arrest!"

CHAPTER TEN

When it came to killing, he liked to be careful. He liked to make certain that nothing had the chance to go wrong, that there wasn't going to be any chance of being discovered.

He liked to watch his victims. Currently, he was watching a young woman named Aurora. She was meeting a friend for lunch and he was watching both of them from a table in the corner. He was being subtle about it, of course. Too much attention too soon would just be obvious. It would be the kind of thing that the cops might pick up on security footage, or that might even make the young woman in question report him to the cops.

He couldn't afford that, when he was so close to the completion of everything he'd set out to do.

It was kind of hard not to stare at Aurora, though. She was in her twenties, pretty, red-haired with a pixie-like delight at the world that seemed infectious. She ate delicately, laughed easily, and seemed to be having a generally glorious day.

He wasn't sure if he should be happy about that or not. Should someone who was going to die so soon be happy? Was it a good thing that she got to have one last good day, or was that somehow wrong? Shouldn't the shadow of what was going to happen weigh on all of this even if she didn't know what was going to happen? The universe knew. There should be some sign of what was going to come.

Or maybe this happiness *was* a sign, a sign to him. A sign that this was the perfect victim, at the perfect moment. That he'd made the right choice.

When Aurora and her friend finished their meals, he waited for them to leave and then followed a little way behind. He watched them split up, continuing to follow Aurora, learning as much about her as he could. He liked to know the routines of those he took perfectly before he snatched them. He liked to know that when the moment came, there would be no complications, nothing that would attract unwanted attention or ruin the moment.

As he followed behind Aurora, he found his hand sliding inside his jacket, looking for the usual, reassuring contact with the knife he kept there. That knife was so bright and so sharp that it must feel like being stabbed with a shaft of moonlight. He liked to think that it was so sharp, those he chose barely even felt it in the moments before they died.

He liked to think that, because pain wasn't what any of this required. Death, yes, but not pain.

Inevitably, he found his thoughts drifting toward the unconscionable as his fingers brushed the hilt of the knife. He found himself thinking about just how easy it would be for him to find a quiet spot somewhere along this street and simply sink the knife into Aurora's unresisting heart as he passed, leaving her dead before she or anyone else around her even knew what was happening.

He could do it. It would be easy. Almost without thinking about it, he found himself quickening his steps, closing the distance between himself and her, the knife drawn now but held flat against his forearm where no one would see it. It would be so simple, so why not just—

No!

At the last minute, he forced himself to veer around Aurora, stepping past her and moving on while he slid his knife back into its sheath. This wasn't how he did things, not here in daylight, where the moon could not see his work. He wasn't some animal who killed at random. Every death he brought about had purpose, meaning.

He forced himself to keep walking, angry with himself as he always was at this point for how close he'd come to breaking his own rules. A quiet kill in the middle of the street wasn't the point of all of this. It wouldn't achieve any of the things that he wanted to achieve. It wouldn't fit the pattern that he'd worked so hard to create, and that even now, the press were only just starting to pick up on.

No, he would do what he always did. He would wait. He would prepare. He would leave Aurora safe until tonight, until the moon stared down at his efforts. He would be there to make sure that this happened in the right place, at the right time. Aurora could go about her day safely for now.

Tonight, though… tonight she would die.

CHAPTER ELEVEN

Maya sat in one of the Chesterford PD's interrogation rooms, looking across a metal table at Samuel Lawrentine, or Sammy Christopher, or whatever his name was. Which brought Maya to her first question.

"What's your name? Your real name?"

"I don't have anything to say to you," Samuel said.

Marco was standing at the side of the room, looking at Samuel levelly. "How about we contact your most recent employer to ask them which of your names they'd prefer to know you by."

That got a brief look of worry from Samuel as he tried to work out just how much trouble he was in, and for what.

"So, do you want to tell us why one moment you were driving around playing the bad-boy boyfriend to Lola Marques and the next you're Samuel Lawrentine, mid-level staffer at an important consultancy firm?" Maya asked.

Samuel just sat there, staring back at her with obvious hostility.

"Your record provides a couple of obvious answers," Maya said. She was determined not to let it go too easily. Not when his minor criminal activities potentially provided a motive for him to have killed Lola Marques. "You're a known con artist. That suggests that you got a job with the consultancy firm either because it would help you to get to their clients' money or because you felt that you could use the position to your advantage in some other way."

"Maybe I turned my life around and got a real job after what happened to Lola," Samuel countered.

Coming from someone else, Maya might have believed that, but from him? Especially after he'd run?

Marco seemed to pick up on the same point. "If you turned your life around, you wouldn't feel the need to run as soon as the FBI showed up."

"Force of habit," Samuel said. "I forgot that I didn't have anything to worry about. I'm telling you, I'm an upstanding member of society now."

Maya wasn't sure why he was even trying that particular line. It obviously wasn't going to work with her or Marco. Every instinct

Maya had said that Samuel here was guilty of *something*. It was just a question now of whether that was the murders she and Marco had been sent to investigate and, if so, whether they could prove that.

"So when we talk to the consultancy firm about the qualifications you claimed on your resume, those will all be things you actually have?" Marco asked.

Samuel spread his hands. "Well, everyone stretches the truth a little with that kind of thing."

None of this seemed to be affecting him. There was certainly no sense of shame there for him, and that caught Maya's attention. Was she talking to a psychopath? Someone who simply couldn't conceive of anything he'd done as wrong? That would be exactly the kind of response she might expect from the killer.

"You stretch the truth about a lot of things, Samuel," Marco said. "So what happens when we start running your prints? How many different names come up?"

That got a brief flicker of reaction, showed a brief crack in the mask that Samuel was keeping up. It suggested that when the Chesterford PD really did finish running his prints, they were going to find crimes under all kinds of other names.

"You need to start talking to us, Samuel," Maya said. "Staying silent isn't going to help you now. You think that if you just say nothing, we're going to let you go without looking too closely at you, the way the Chesterford PD did after Lola died."

She paused for a moment, watching the small flicker of reaction that said that was *exactly* what he thought was going to happen.

"But we're the FBI," Maya went on. "And we aren't going to stop that easily. We'll dig into every facet of your life. We'll find everything you've ever done. Being quiet won't change that. So talk to us about Lola."

"What about her?" Samuel asked.

"What was the idea when you got close to her?" Marco asked. "Were you trying to con her family? Establish some identity that you could use for something else?"

Samuel shrugged. Again, Maya got the feeling that they'd hit close to home with him.

"So what happened then?" Maya asked. "Did she find out about you? Did she realize that you weren't who you said you were? Was that why you killed her?"

That got a brief flash of anger from Samuel. Not guilt or grief or sadness at the death, just anger.

"I never killed anyone!" He slammed a hand into the table. "The cops tried to frame me for this before. They couldn't find any evidence, and you can't either."

The problem was that he had a point. They didn't have any physical evidence linking him to the crime scenes. All Maya could do now was to try to get some kind of confession, and that was looking less likely by the moment.

"But you weren't able to give the police an alibi," Maya said. "You skipped town as soon as you could, you changed your name. We'll hold you in relation to whatever con you're trying to pull at Verison-Smythe. That will give us plenty of time to pull apart your home, your car, every facet of your life. If there's a trace of DNA to be found linking you to either of the two victims…"

"Two victims?" Samuel said, and there seemed to be the briefest moment of actual emotion there as surprise came through on his face.

"Where were you last night?" Maya asked.

Samuel looked as though he wasn't going to answer.

"Where?" Marco demanded, obviously not letting go of it.

Then Samuel smiled to himself, smugly, as if he were the one in control of all of this. The moment Maya saw that smile, she knew that she'd gone wrong somewhere.

"I was at a party," Samuel said. "One for the firm. I was there all evening. You'll be able to find plenty of photos of me there and people who remember me."

Maya stormed out of the interrogation room, just because the look on Samuel's face was too much to bear. She stood outside it, taking deep breaths, trying to contain the anger and frustration she felt after using up so much time on someone who had proved to be such a waste of that time.

Marco was beside her then, a hand on her shoulder. "There's still a chance that he's lying and he wasn't at the party."

"He will have been," Maya said. "He'll have been there or he wouldn't say it. He'll know that this is his only way out of all of this, and he'll *also* know that we'll check it."

"Is that what we do next?" Marco asked.

Maya shook her head. She wasn't going to give Samuel another second of her time. "We'll have the local PD do it. We need to find another angle that will work, another way of looking for the killer."

The only question was what that might be. Samuel had seemed like a promising lead, but now that it clearly wasn't him, who could it be?

Were there other connections between Lola and Helene that might lead them to someone?

Maya found a desk and grabbed her laptop, determined to keep looking. Yet something stopped her from just diving back into the two young women's social media.

"This isn't the way we find the killer," Maya said.

"What do you mean?" Marco asked, taking a seat alongside her.

"I mean that this doesn't *feel* like some guy that they both knew who slipped over into murder after they found out some secret, or who is angry with them because of some personal issue," Maya said. "This doesn't feel like any kind of ordinary murder. The way the victims were posed… *that's* what makes all of this unique, so who would do something like that?"

"And have they done this before?" Marco said. "The murders were highly professional. They didn't leave any evidence behind. They set everything up precisely."

"But is it possible that another murder like this could be missed?" Maya pointed out. "Something like this, it would stick in the minds of the cops, wouldn't it?"

"Not if they thought they were looking at something else," Marco said. "Remember, they decided that this was a Moonlight Killer murder because it was on the full moon."

They'd seen that before, in other places, where a murder had been assumed to be the work of the Moonlight Killer and so no one had connected it to others that didn't quite fit the pattern. Was that really possible here, though? With something as obvious as a posed body?

"It has to be worth trying," Marco said.

Maya nodded. It was a better option than trying to get more out of someone like Samuel, at least. She started to look through the Chesterford PD's files, trying to find an answer.

She started by searching for murders, but Chesterford was still big enough that there had been several of those over the last couple of years. Some were clearly not relevant, ones where people had been shot or stabbed in robberies gone wrong or killed by their partners in incidents of domestic abuse.

She looked just for ones that involved stabbing, but that still gave her several files to look through. And she *had* to look through the files, one by one, because she didn't trust that this would be something that could be done just through computer searches.

So Maya read through the details of each murder, one after another, trying to push back the thought that each one was a loss to someone, a pain that was impossible to heal.

She had to look, because she had to be sure that there were no others that fit this killer's pattern. Did there have to be, though? Maybe there really were just these two murders. Maybe that was enough,

Maya had to keep going, though, looking for any murder in which the victim had been posed after death, in any way. That narrowed things down, but still not quite enough.

"Maya, I think I've found something," Marco said. He was also looking through files. Maya had been so caught up in her own research that she'd barely paid any attention to what he was doing.

"What have you found?" Maya asked.

"Here, there's a file that's been wrongly labeled as a gang killing. It was right on the edge of the city's jurisdiction. Look for yourself."

Maya went to stand behind him, looking over his shoulder at his screen. There, she saw the crime scene photographs. Those showed a woman tied to a post, her arms stretched out at angles.

It might have been a prototype for the other kills. The fine details weren't quite the same, but the moment Maya saw it, she knew that this was the work of the same man.

"Aisling Byrne," Maya said. The file said that she'd been killed a month and a half ago. That meant that she was the killer's oldest victim, or at least the earliest that they had found. If he'd messed up anywhere, it would likely be with her.

CHAPTER TWELVE

As she and Marco drove out toward the spot where Aisling Byrne had died, she read through the files on the murder, trying to get as much information as possible before she arrived.

Aisling had been twenty-three, young and pretty, pale and red-haired. In the pictures Maya found of her, she had a faraway look like she couldn't quite focus on the world around her. She'd been an artist, working in an array of media.

Maya looked at her social media, trying to get a sense of who this young woman had been. She didn't appear to be friends online with either Helene Gretting or Lola Marques, but Maya hadn't expected that to be the case. Maya didn't think that this was about some personal conflict, a relationship gone wrong or someone who had found out about a criminal's activities and paid the price for it.

The posing of the bodies said that it was something else, something darker and more dangerous. To Maya, this said that it wasn't a killer trying to achieve some simple aim, trying to clear up some kind of mess or eliminate witnesses to a crime. This was a serial killer to whom all of this meant something, who was doing things this way for a reason.

That was a part of why Maya and Marco were driving down to the spot where Aisling Byrne had been found: because if it helped them to understand why the killer was doing all of this, they might have a better chance of working out *who* had done this.

It was also one of the reasons Maya was looking deeper into Aisling's life, trying to find out what she could about the young woman. This was the first time—the first they knew about anyway—that the murderer in this case had killed someone, and the first time was often more meaningful for serial killers. They might go on to kill strangers at random, but the first person they hurt was often someone close to them, someone who meant something in the context of their lives.

The first murders were also the ones where they were the most likely to make mistakes. Which made it far more frustrating as Maya went through the file and saw that the investigation into this case had been haphazard at best.

The first officers on the scene had been from the neighboring sheriff's department, since the crime scene had been right on the limits of the jurisdiction between one and another. They'd been the ones to assume that it was related to some problems with gangs and drugs that they'd had in the area, and somehow, that had translated into an investigation that had been badly conducted. The evidence collection at the scene had been poor, and there was no chance of getting back anything that had been missed there.

Even so, Maya needed to see the spot, just for the chance to get into the killer's head. She wanted to know why he'd chosen to kill out here, in a spot out beyond the town, in an open field with a stretch of woodland at one end of it. It was away from the road, so that she and Marco had to park at the side of the highway and then walk.

"Why here?" Marco asked, looking around. "It's a long way from anywhere. How was the body even found?"

"Another anonymous tip," Maya said. "That was another part of why the cops who attended assumed that it was gang related. They thought it was criminals sending a message."

"It was," Marco said. "Just not in the way that they thought."

He had a point. The killer had called in his work on each occasion, had displayed his victims openly, taking the time to pose them carefully, as if the way that people saw them mattered to him almost more than anything else. Even with this first murder, he'd wanted the police to see.

Which brought Maya back to her original question.

"Why here? If he wanted people to see, why leave Aisling Byrne out in the middle of nowhere? A park like the one he left Helene Gretting in, I can understand. People would always come by. There was always a chance for them to take photographs or for reporters to see. Out here… I'm not sure if this murder even made the news."

Maya ran a search for that, wanting to check. There had been a brief mention, but it was nothing compared to the scale of the coverage for the two more recent murders. Would that lack of coverage have angered the killer? Would it have pushed him to change his methods to try to ensure that more people saw his next efforts?

"How did he even get Aisling here?" Marco asked. He gestured to the open expanse of the field. "This isn't somewhere that she would have come willingly with a stranger."

"Suggesting either that she knew her killer or that he kidnapped her first, subdued her, and then brought her here."

"We know that he was able to pose his other victims before he killed them," Marco said. "That suggests that he found a way to subdue them. Does the coroner's report show defensive wounds that might mean she was attacked before the murder?"

Maya shook her head as she checked over the report. "But there *were* traces of drugs in her system. He drugged her before he killed her."

The only problem was that it didn't do anything to say for sure whether Aisling Byrne had known the man who killed her. It was possible that someone had lured her here to kill her and then drugged her to make it easier. It was possible that someone had drugged her earlier and then brought her here. It was impossible to say.

Maya looked out over the field, trying to guess what had made the killer pick this place.

"The kill wasn't under the full moon," she said. "But it was still at night. Maybe that's important to the killer."

"Or maybe it's just the easiest time to do something like this without risking someone seeing it," Marco pointed out.

Anywhere else, Maya would have agreed, but out here, there didn't seem to be any obvious way for a passerby to spot what was going on. There didn't even seem to be any passersby.

"This place is remote enough that I'm not sure if he'd need the cover of darkness," Maya said. "Although maybe he was just being cautious. I'm interested in why he picked here. Was it just because it was remote? And, if so, why switch to places within Chesterford?"

"Maybe he's taking greater risks for the thrill of it," Marco suggested.

That was a possibility. Some killers did that, escalating from kill to kill, trying to see what they could get away with, trying to be more and more outrageous, almost daring the authorities to stop them. Some even *wanted* to be stopped. Was that this killer?

Maya hoped not, because if she and Marco were dealing with a killer like that, there would only be an acceleration to whatever pattern he had. He would kill more and more people faster and faster, until they stopped him.

But to do that, to work out who had done this, they needed to understand *why* the killer was murdering people the way he was.

"Why is he posing them like this?" Maya asked. That was the part of all of this that stood out. The part that had let them connect the three murders in the first place. Three women, all killed in the same way, all *posed* in the same way.

That had to be significant. It had to mean something to the killer, or why would he do it? Why would he go to the trouble of bringing them to a specific location while they were still alive before he killed them? Why would he construct wood and metal frames to hold them in the perfect position?

"It's almost like art," Maya said.

"Art?" Marco asked, sounding like he didn't quite believe it, perhaps because of the brutality of it all.

"I know it's dark, I know it's twisted, but that's not what matters," Maya said. "What matters is that the *killer* thinks it's art."

"Do you really think that's what he's thinking?" Marco asked.

Maya paused to consider it. She felt as though there was something there, as though this might be an answer. It certainly seemed to fit with the facts of this first murder.

"I think so, and it even fits this first choice of victim. Aisling was an artist. Look at her social media."

Maya pulled it up so that Marco could see. There were pictures there of works across a variety of media, as if Aisling were stretching herself, trying to find what worked best for her. Maya didn't know much about art, but there seemed to be a hint of talent there, like she was on the verge of becoming much better. Some of the pieces shortly before her death were darker, though, with a rougher edge to them and more violent symbolism.

"I see what you mean," Marco said. "Wait, scroll back a little. Who's that?"

There were pictures of Aisling there, around the time of those more violent-looking pieces, with a tall, pale man around her age who dressed like a goth in all black with plenty of leather and a lot of silver jewelry. Maya was about to say that it wasn't anyone who mattered, but then she caught the captions to some of the photographs.

Me with Larsen at the opening of his show.

Larsen with his latest work.

Maya started to look through the posts in more detail and quickly realized that Aisling had briefly been in a relationship with this "Larsen," whose full name seemed to be Larsen Reynolds.

That didn't mean much until Maya started looking at some of the works in the background of the posts, which seemed to be depictions of people in states of agony, twisted and tortured almost beyond recognition.

That was enough to send Maya off looking for the work of Larsen Reynolds. He had a website with pictures of some of his pieces, and the paintings were disturbing enough, but it was the section on sculpture that made Maya truly stop and stare.

The description at the top of the page said it all:

Larsen likes to incorporate the visceral and the real in his work in a reminder of the fundamental mortality and fragility of the human form. As a result, his practice has often incorporated human blood, teeth, and other body parts, challenging our instinctive reactions and calling into question the ways in which we separate ourselves from the reality of life and death.

"An artist boyfriend who sounds like a real piece of work," Marco said, looking over Maya's shoulder. She saw him typing into his phone. "Plus, he has a record. Minor stuff mostly, some violence. Looks like the most recent arrest was for the battery of an ex-girlfriend, but she dropped the charges."

"And the cops didn't go after him following Aisling's murder?" Maya said. She found that hard to believe. Had they really been so fixated on the story they'd been telling themselves about her death that they hadn't checked out her violent ex-boyfriend?

Apparently not, and it was possible that decision had cost two more women their lives, because, to Maya, Larsen Reynolds seemed like a great candidate to be the killer they were looking for.

CHAPTER THIRTEEN

As they drove back into town, Maya heard her new phone ringing. One look at the screen told her that it was Agent Swift. On another occasion, that might have been enough to get Maya to ignore the call, but now that she and Marco were nominally attached to Agent Swift's task force hunting the Moonlight Killer, she didn't have much of a choice about it.

"Agent Grey, give me an update on your progress," Swift said without preamble when Maya answered.

"We've arrived in the town and we're looking at suspects. We're not dealing with one murder anymore, but with a series of three so far by the same killer, all pretty much identical."

"Do you have any leads at the moment?" Swift asked.

"With the way the bodies were posed, we're looking into a local artist who has a history of using body parts in his work."

"Body parts? And there I thought I'd heard everything in this job. Is there any specific connection to the victims?"

Maya didn't like having to go through her whole chain of reasoning on this with Swift, but if it bought her the chance to do her job, then she was willing to go along with it.

"He's the ex-boyfriend of the first victim and he has a criminal record that includes violence towards another ex-girlfriend."

"Sounds like a real scumbag. Okay, keep going."

Maya could have left the call at that, but there was something else she needed to ask.

"Agent Swift? Why exactly did you back me and Marco back in the disciplinary hearing?"

There was a pause on the other end of the line as Agent Swift considered her words.

"For more than two years now, my job has been to try to catch the Moonlight Killer. You've gotten closer to achieving that in the last few weeks than I did in all that time. I care about catching this bastard, and if Harris can't see how you make it possible to get to him, then he isn't helping."

Maya was grateful that Swift was willing to let her keep going with all of this, but at the same time, she knew that Swift had the potential to make the end of this more complicated. Maya was sure that Swift wanted to do everything she could to end this well, but would her attempts to get to the Moonlight Killer prove just as dangerous to Maya's sister Megan as Harris's had?

No, it was better not to think about that part.

"For now, we need to focus on this case," Maya said. "Succeeding in this is the only way that we get to the Moonlight Killer."

It was also the only way that they got Megan back.

"I know you're planning to do this your own way to make sure that you get your sister back," Agent Swift said.

"After Harris, can you blame me?"

"I get why you have that instinct. But remember that the FBI is a team. We're here to back you up. And Grey… if you want to try to take the Moonlight Killer alone, you'd better not lose him."

"I won't," Maya assured her. She hoped that she could back that promise up, because if she couldn't, then her sister was dead.

"We're here," Marco said, which gave Maya an excuse to hang up.

She found that they were outside what appeared to be an old warehouse, one that seemed almost abandoned, like no one had touched the exterior of it in years. Several of the windows were boarded up, while there was graffiti on the outside. It took Maya a moment or two to realize that these weren't the usual tags and random scrawls of passing graffiti artists, but a series of interlocking murals by different artists, as if someone had brought them in one after another to decorate the exterior of the warehouse.

"We're sure this is the right place?" Maya asked.

Marco shrugged. "This is the address that's on his website, and it matches the DMV."

Even knowing that, it was still hard to believe that anyone lived there, even an artist. There was only one way to be sure. Maya got out of the car and headed for the door, hammering on it since there didn't seem to be a bell.

There was no answer from inside, but as Maya listened closely, she thought she could hear the sound of metal music somewhere inside, muted, but definitely there.

Maya knocked harder on the door. "Larsen Reynolds! Open up! This is the FBI!"

She thought she heard the music stop. There was a pause and the length of that pause started to make her nervous. Was it possible that Larsen was taking the opportunity to run, taking some back way out of the warehouse? Maya took a step back, almost ready to kick the door open while sending Marco around to cover the rear of the place. If Larsen was the killer, then wouldn't it make sense for him to run?

Even as Maya thought that, though, the door swung open, revealing a tall man dressed all in black, dark hair slicked back and pale makeup covering his face. He looked at Maya and Marco balefully, his eyes hidden behind dark glasses.

"What do you want?" he demanded.

Maya frowned at that. Couldn't he guess? His ex-girlfriend had been killed only a month and a half ago. Why did he *think* the FBI was knocking on his door?

"We're here to talk to you about Aisling," Maya said.

Maya barely saw any reaction to that.

"And what makes you think that I want to talk about her?" Larsen demanded.

Maya didn't have time for any games now. "You have a choice: we can talk about her here, or we can talk about her down at the local police precinct."

That got a reaction, in the form of a brief flicker of anger. Then Larsen stepped back, gesturing extravagantly for them to step inside.

"Very well. It is always… amusing to have law enforcement here. Your tastes are always so… predictable."

Maya stepped inside with Marco behind her. For a moment or two after she did so, all she could do was stare.

The interior had been remodeled in a way that the exterior hadn't, creating a huge studio space that was obviously designed to allow Larsen to continue his work. It was divided into different areas, one given over to sleeping, another to a kitchen, while others seemed to be designed for painting, woodworking, metalwork…

It was hard to take in all of that when examples of Larsen's work were set out around the studio. There were paintings splashed with dark reds that were clearly blood, because blood bags hung nearby, ready for use. There were sculptures that seemed to include lengths of human bone almost at random, replacing sections of otherwise metal or wooden figures. There were books that looked leather-bound, but memories of the artist's website told her that Larsen had a whole series where he'd worked with human skin.

Maya had to swallow her disgust at the sight of it all, reminding herself that she'd seen far worse. She'd seen people who had been murdered, had seen the aftermath of battles back in the days when she'd been in military intelligence.

"Ah, it's always good seeing the shock and disgust of those who can't understand what they're seeing," Larsen said.

"And what *are* we seeing?" Marco asked in a tight tone that suggested that he wasn't any happier about the contents of the studio than Maya was.

"My work," Larsen said. "A true expression. An expression that *means* something. Those things that you're feeling right now… isn't it the purpose of art to force the viewer to feel? To shock those who look at it out of the mundanity of their lives?"

Maya got the feeling that the artist liked being in control of this situation. He liked the fact that his work was unsettling her and Marco. She needed to bring the focus back to the case she and Marco were working.

"Tell us about Aisling," Maya said.

"What about her?"

"Doesn't it bother you that she's dead?" Marco asked, obviously reacting to the coldness of Larsen's response.

Larsen looked at him as if he'd just said something that didn't make any sense. "Of course you wouldn't get it. Death isn't something to be feared. Death is simply the next step in the human journey. If we don't confront it, how can we become all that we can be?"

"And did Aisling confront death when she was with you?" Maya asked. "I've seen her work."

She heard Larsen snort. "She tried, but ultimately she didn't have what it took. She got scared and she ran away from the art."

"From the art?" Maya asked. "Or from you?"

Larsen just smiled. "You're here to question me, so ask your questions. Ask what you really want to ask."

"Did you have anything to do with her death?" Maya asked.

"No, of course not," Larsen said. Maya heard him sigh. "You people are all so predictable. I work with body parts, so of course I must be some kind of killer."

"Not just a killer," Marco said. "A serial killer."

That seemed to catch Larsen's interest. "A serial killer?"

"Two more women have been killed in the same way as Aisling," Maya said. "So yes, we want to talk to you. Because these women were posed like they were sculptures. Like something *you* might do, Mr. Reynolds."

Larsen seemed a little irritated by that.

"Do you know what it's like? Do you know how often I get cops sniffing around here? Everything I do is perfectly legal. Every sample of tissue, bone, or blood I use is donated by individuals who want to be a part of artistic greatness. Every instance is documented, every sample is traceable. That's a *part* of the art. My work is at least part memorial to the dead."

He made it sound as if he were doing some kind of public service. More than that, he sounded to Maya as if he genuinely believed it. He certainly sounded upset by the idea that he might have done anything illegal.

But that wasn't enough for Maya. It would be easy for the killer to pretend that he had nothing to do with any of this. Maybe Larsen had grown tired of how little of a body he was able to use at once. Maybe he'd decided to go further, to step over every boundary that remained even for him.

"Where were you last night?" Maya asked.

"Ah, you're looking for an alibi?" Larsen said. He took out his phone, showing Maya a series of pictures. He was in most of them, standing by a series of sculptures in the middle of what appeared to be a party. "I was in LA until late. A wealthy art collector bought a couple of my pieces. It's so rare to run into someone who truly appreciates real art. I only flew back this morning."

"And you have your ticket for that flight?" Marco asked.

"Of course."

Which meant that there was no way that Larsen could have killed Helene Gretting. And *that* meant that he probably hadn't killed either of the other victims. They were wasting their time here.

Maya felt an immediate wash of frustration, quickly followed by a kind of relief, because at least it meant that they could get out of there. She turned to walk back to the door.

"Can I… can I see them?" Larsen said.

Maya turned back to him with a frown. "See them?"

"See what they did? See the… crime scenes? If this is sculpture, if someone is making art with the dead… I have to see it."

He made it sound as though it was as inevitable as water flowing downhill, but Maya had no intention of sharing crime scene photographs with someone who didn't need to see them, especially not someone like this.

"I can help," Larsen said. "I know more artists than you. Especially those who do this work. If this is by anyone I know, you'll have caught your killer."

He made it sound so simple, so easy. The worst part was that he had a point. As ghoulish as his interest seemed, he *might* be able to help.

Gritting her teeth, Maya pulled up images of the three crime scenes on her phone, showing them to Larsen one after another. He stared at them with a frown.

"Well, I can tell you one thing," he said after a couple of seconds with a note of disdain.

"What's that?"

"This isn't art."

That caught Maya by surprise.

"Do you just mean that it isn't good, or—"

"I mean that it isn't *art*," Larsen said. "Look at the three. Look at the lack of variation, the mechanical simplicity of it all. There's nothing artistic about this. It isn't about display, or about the effect it has on the viewer. This… this is just *engineering*."

He made that sound as if it were the worst thing possible.

"The person who did this isn't creating anything new, isn't trying to affect your senses. They're just copying something, trying to make something functional."

"How can you be sure of that?" Marco demanded.

"Do you think I don't know art when I see it?" Larsen said. "Besides, I would know if this were the work of anyone in the field, and it doesn't match up with anyone I've heard of. No, this isn't art. Which means that it isn't interesting."

"The deaths of three women aren't interesting?" Maya said. She still couldn't understand how someone could be so cold about this.

Larsen just shrugged. "You're boring me now. If there's nothing else, I have *real* art to create."

Maya turned for the door, grateful to finally get out of there.

CHAPTER FOURTEEN

It was starting to get dark by the time Maya and Marco returned to the Chesterford PD, the shifts of the police officers switching over as the city moved into night. Maya felt as though she could feel the tension in the building. Obviously, everyone there knew that the serial killer struck at night, so they were waiting for the possibility that someone might call in with an anonymous tip leading to another body.

Of course, there was no reason why there should be. This was a killer whose kills to date had been spread out over a couple of months. Yet it was still impossible to escape the worry that it *might* happen.

Maybe that was at least partly down to the Moonlight Killer's deadline, too. It had Maya on edge.

"I take it that we're pushing through the night without stopping to rest?" Marco asked.

Maya nodded. He knew as well as she did that there was no time for sleep. "Given the midnight deadline, we can't afford to waste a single minute, even for a nap."

"Are you sure you're going to be able to handle that?" Marco asked. "Remember, you were shot."

"So were you," Maya countered.

"Which is how I know just how much this must be taking out of you."

Maya had to admit that Marco had a point. Running around all day after leads had used up a lot of her energy, so that she was mostly keeping going on adrenaline now. Her side ached from the effort she'd put in, particularly chasing after Samuel Lawrentine earlier. Yet she also knew that stopping wasn't an option, not now.

"In just another day, my sister will die if we don't come up with an answer in this case," Maya said. "We have to keep going. We can't even take a few minutes away from this."

Marco looked as though he might argue for a moment or two, but then seemed to realize that Maya was right. He nodded, then put a hand on her shoulder. "All right, but don't push so hard that you hurt yourself. I don't want to have to visit you in the hospital again."

"If getting Megan back alive costs me another trip to the hospital, then it will be worth it," Maya insisted.

"And if you end up in the morgue rather than the hospital?" Marco asked.

Maya wasn't sure what to say to that. Would she trade her life for her sister's? If the only way to take down the Moonlight Killer and save Megan involved Maya's death, would she do it?

"We're all going to come through this," Maya insisted. She was dodging the question, but the truth was that she didn't have any good answers right then. She didn't want to argue with Marco about the extent to which she would put herself in danger to save her sister, but she knew that he would want to do everything he could to keep Maya safe.

"I hope so," Marco replied.

The two of them took seats at a couple of borrowed desks in the department.

"So, now what?" Marco asked.

"I want you to take a minute to check the alibis of the two suspects we've looked at already," Maya said. "Neither one of them is exactly trustworthy, so let's make sure that there isn't a hole in one of their alibis that would let them still be the killer."

Marco nodded. "I can do that."

"After that, start looking deeper into the three victims, just in case there's some hidden connection between them that we haven't been able to spot so far."

"You think there will be?" Marco asked with a slight frown that suggested he wasn't confident about it.

"I don't know," Maya admitted. "Given that he takes his victims alive to the places where he kills them and that they don't seem to be places they would normally go, that suggests that he's stalking them beforehand to find the perfect opportunity. Combine that with the fact that all three victims have been young women around the same age and that suggests that he isn't picking his victims at random."

"So I'm not necessarily looking for any sign that the three knew one another, just anything they might have had in common?" Marco said.

Maya nodded. "I know it's a long shot, but maybe there will be something there that suggests why he's picking one victim over another. Something that might let us get ahead of him on this."

"All right," Marco said. "What will you be doing while I'm working on that?"

"I'll start by looking at more artists," Maya said. "Just because Larsen Reynolds doesn't recognize this as someone's style, that doesn't mean that there's no artist out there it could be."

"Good luck."

Maya hoped it wouldn't come down to luck, just to her ability to research. She set to work, looking for artists who might work with human body parts. It meant having to steel herself to cope with the images that came up, because the artists who worked like that seemed to be deliberately trying to shock or disgust the audience a lot of the time. Trying to challenge their reactions toward their own mortality, she guessed someone like Larsen would say.

The problem was that, while there were a few such artists out there, they weren't *here*. They weren't in Chesterford. As far as Maya could see, the only artist who did that kind of work in the town was Larsen Reynolds, and they'd already eliminated him as a suspect. At least, unless Marco somehow managed to break what seemed like an ironclad alibi.

Maya broadened her search a little, looking for locally produced art with generally darker themes, hoping that she might stumble across something that depicted exactly the kind of structure the killer had been leaving his victims tied to. It was possible, wasn't it, that a killer might draw or paint the image he had in his head before he went on to try to recreate it in real life?

Maya started to look through as many art pieces as possible produced in the local area. She started with any artists connected to either Aisling Byrne or Larsen Reynolds, still working on the principle that there might be a link to Aisling as the first victim. Maybe someone who admired Larsen's work and decided that she had hurt him by breaking up with him?

Maya found plenty of dark and disturbing art out there, but nothing that was an exact match for the crime scenes. There was nothing out there that might have served as a blueprint for it.

It was getting later. Looking through pieces of art one by one took time and Maya wasn't sure if she and Marco had that time. The murders seemed to be at irregular intervals, which meant that there was no way of knowing whether the killer would strike again tonight or leave it another month.

Maya's instincts said that he would strike again as soon as he felt able to. A killer like this didn't stop or slow down; he only escalated. For all she knew, he might already be out there, stalking another victim, ready to tie her to a structure and kill her in the name of art.

Or maybe *not* in the name of art. What was it that Larsen had said? That none of the murders were about art, because they were all too closely identical? There was no variation, no sense of personality, and thus no art.

A part of Maya suspected that the artist was just being snobbish about what he'd seen, that when he said that it wasn't art, he simply meant that the killer's efforts were *bad* art. After all, weren't there identical series of sculptures out there? Hadn't some artists made the same thing over and over in the hope of finding perfection? In that sense, the killer's efforts could simply reflect his own dissatisfaction with his "work," killing again and again in the hope of finally making things perfect, when they could never *be* perfect.

That was one potential explanation, but Maya found herself wondering if there wasn't an alternative. Was it possible that Larsen was right? Was it possible that this *wasn't* art, but was instead some kind of construction with a practical purpose?

What, though? Maya stared at the crime scene photographs, trying to make some kind of sense of it all. Assume that the killer was trying to engineer something functional that incorporated the bodies of his victims. What possible function could it have?

There were no moving parts, no sense of a mechanism that could be adjusted or changed. If anything, the purpose of the structures the killer tied his victims to seemed to be to make sure that they *wouldn't* change, making sure that they stayed in exactly the same position regardless of what happened around them.

Was that important? Was the positioning the key to all of this? If so, why had the women been left in three such different places? A field, a park, the side of a river… the only connection seemed to be that they'd all been left out in nature, open to the night air.

Briefly, Maya found herself looking at funerary practices. She vaguely remembered hearing somewhere that there were historical cultures that had left their dead out in the open air for scavengers. Yet, as far as she could see, such cultures either left the dead at ground level in some natural place or left them up on raised platforms. The killer wasn't copying that.

No, Maya couldn't shake the feeling that he was trying to shape his victims into something useful, something that achieved a particular purpose. What purpose, though, could require them to be left out in the places where they had been found, at night?

Maya hunched over the desk, trying to force herself to think in spite of the tiredness that was starting to creep into every fiber of her being.

She wasn't going to stop now; wasn't going to stop until she had her sister back. She just had to find the right way to think about all this.

What was unusual about the murders? The fact that the killer tied his victims in place, yes, but also the fact that he brought them there to die in a particular time and place.

Were those times and places important? Maya couldn't see how right now. She tried plotting out the three murders on a map, and it seemed to her that they all fit onto the same gentle curve, but she wasn't sure if that was enough information to get any further in the case. She needed more.

There was only one more piece of information about the case that stood out: the anonymous tip-off. Why, in every case, had the killer taken the risk of calling in the murder to the police? It was a major risk on his part, because there was always a chance that the police could trace the call and catch up to him before he got away.

Why didn't he just leave the bodies to be found by whoever passed by in the morning? Unless… unless he needed them to be found then, at a particular time.

Maya found herself thinking about time then. She looked at the victims, and at the contraptions that they were tied to. Didn't those look faintly like sundials? Only they couldn't be sundials, because the murders took place at night.

Maya went online, trying to research a possible solution.

"Moondials!" She said it loud enough that she saw Marco start. Had he begun to fall asleep at his desk?

"Moon what?" Marco said.

"Moondials," Maya repeated. "He's turning his victims into instruments that potentially let people tell the time by the moon, the same way that a sundial would with the sun, casting a shadow to indicate the time in the moonlight. It explains why they were tied in a precise position, and why they were left out in the open air."

"Are those common?" Marco asked.

Maya shook her head. "From what I've been able to find, they mostly crop up in lunar gardens to indicate the time particular flowers should open, but they aren't very accurate."

"So who would want to make an inaccurate timepiece that works by the moon?" Marco asked.

To Maya there was only one answer to that.

"Someone obsessed with the moon."

CHAPTER FIFTEEN

The moon. Could this really all be about the moon? The more Maya thought about it, the more likely it seemed to be true. The Moonlight Killer had sent them out, not just to clear away other murders that muddied the waters when it came to his own killing spree, but to sweep away any rivals to him, to lock up other serial killers who killed by the light of the moon.

A part of Maya hated that, hated being used to do the Moonlight Killer's dirty work. Yet, at the same time, it had meant being able to take multiple killers off the street who otherwise would have gone free, and who might still have been killing more victims. Maya wasn't so arrogant that she believed that no one else could have done her job, but in several cases, she knew that the police simply hadn't been looking for any suspects beyond the Moonlight Killer.

She needed to focus on this case, though. It was getting late and they still didn't have any good suspects. The killer could already be out there, stalking another victim.

"Who would want to build a moondial?" Maya asked Marco.

"To tell the time by the moon? Maybe a gardener, or an astronomer. You said it yourself, they would have to be obsessed with the moon."

An astronomer. That sounded plausible. Someone for whom the exact positioning of astronomical bodies mattered almost more than anything. Where could they find out about an obsessive astronomer?

Maya's first instinct was to call local colleges to see if there were any members of their staff who met that description. The problem with that was that everyone who worked at a place like that was likely to be home by now, not sitting waiting to answer Maya's call.

She had to think of another way to find astronomers. That meant going online, searching for local astronomy societies, hoping there would be something there to catch her eye.

There was such a society, their website a little clunky and old-fashioned, but with a bunch of links through to everything from major observatories to newsletters on the latest developments in astrophysics.

"You think we're going to find the killer on here?" Marco asked.

"I'm not sure," Maya said. "I'm just looking for anyone connected with all of this who is also a little off, who maybe has a criminal record. Try searching for any local astronomers who might fit that description."

"I'll give it my best shot," Marco said, but it was obvious that he didn't think it was likely that they would find anything like that.

Maya knew that it was a long shot. They knew the general type of person they needed to find, but narrowing that down to a specific individual was harder. It wasn't as if people went out and advertised themselves as dangerous obsessives, fixated on the moon.

She found a forum for the members of the astronomical society and started to look through it, trying to find anyone there who appeared to stand out, anyone who was more argumentative or stranger than the rest. No one stood out, though. That was hardly surprising, since what would a killer look like on a forum like this?

Maya started to search through the forums for anything on moondials, hoping that there might be something there to help her. She was almost surprised when there was a whole thread entitled *Did you hear what happened to the Moondial Professor?*

Just the thought that there might be a professor who was interested in moondials was enough to catch her interest, but when Maya kept reading, she found her suspicions rising.

According to the forum posts, Professor Jacob Corinth had been a professor of astrophysics at one of the big universities. He was best known for a book he'd written on moondials, and it seemed that everyone in the astronomy society had been excited when they heard that he was moving to the town.

That excitement seemed to have lasted until they heard the reasons that he'd been asked to leave his former position.

"Marco, look up a guy named Jacob Corinth," Maya said. "He's a former professor of astrophysics. See what you can find."

"What have *you* found?" Marco asked.

"Just rumors on a message board. That he was fired for harassing his female students. See if there's anything else to find on him."

Maya waited while Marco typed, hoping that there would be something there that would point them in the right direction.

"I've got some stuff on him," Marco said. "He was, as you say, a professor of astrophysics at a prestigious Ivy League university. Most of his research was on boundary effects near black holes, but it seems that everyone knew him best for his work on moondials. He only wrote one book on them, but it was popular. He was getting invited to speak on different lecture circuits."

"What happened then?" Maya asked. She already knew the rumors, but she wanted to see if there was anything else out there that might confirm it all.

"There are a couple of news reports here about him leaving his job, there's an opinion piece on whether professors have too much power over their students, an interview with a young woman who says he made unwanted advances towards her."

All of which suggested that the things Maya had read on the forum were true.

"And he moved to Chesterford as a result," she said. She knew that much from the forums. More than that, she knew the date when he'd done so.

It had only been a couple of months ago. A couple of months, when the first murder in this sequence had been a month and a half back. That timing immediately set alarm bells ringing in Maya's head. Maybe it was a coincidence, but Maya really didn't believe that it could be.

"We're going to need to talk to Jacob Corinth," Maya said.

"That isn't going to be easy."

Maya was already shaking her head. "I don't care about easy right now, Marco. My sister is going to die if we don't get answers. And the killer… he could already be out there, getting ready to kill someone else."

Maya couldn't wait, not tonight, and not with so little time left to investigate this case. She couldn't wait until morning, because who knew if that would give them enough time? She couldn't sit around waiting for the rest of the world to wake up again, couldn't just sleep when there were leads to pursue. She had to go after this, had to try to make progress.

"I'll find an address and call ahead," Marco said.

Maya shook her head even to that. If this was their killer, she didn't want to risk giving him a chance to run. She also didn't want to get there only to find herself met by a lawyer who would stall out their investigation. They would go straight there to try to catch Jacob Corinth off guard. Maybe that would give them the answers they needed.

*

Maya sat in the car outside Jacob Corinth's house, feeling relieved to see that the lights were on there. That suggested that he was home. If he was the killer, that meant that he wasn't out there targeting another victim.

The house was mid-sized, with a relatively expensive-looking car in the driveway. Yet that car was several years old and slightly battered looking, as if Jacob hadn't had the money recently to replace it. Was that a side effect of losing his prestigious position? Was it a sign of how far he'd fallen as a result of the accusations leveled against him by his students?

If so, wouldn't it be reasonable to assume that he would be angry about all of that? In turn, that potentially gave him a strong motive to lash out at other young women, potentially ones who reminded him of the students he'd harassed before.

Maya strode up to the door with Marco, knocking on it sharply. She thought she could hear classical music coming from inside, quickly shut off. Maya knocked again.

"Professor Corinth, this is the FBI. We need to talk to you."

"One minute!" a man's voice called from inside.

Maya looked over to Marco. "Get ready for any sign that he's running."

Marco nodded, moving back from the door to a position where he could get a better view of the side of the house.

Even as he did so, however, the front door opened, revealing a man in his forties, with features that could have been called handsome if the lighting were poor enough, his blond hair still wet, presumably from a shower. He was wearing a white terry cloth robe, while his expression was anything but welcoming.

"What is it?" he demanded. "What is the FBI doing calling on me at this time of the night?"

"We're sorry to disturb you, Professor," Maya said. "But it's urgent. We need to ask you some questions in relation to a case and it couldn't wait. Can we do this inside?"

Professor Corinth looked as though he might shut the door in their faces, but after a few seconds he stepped back to let Maya and Marco pass.

"What's this about?" he demanded, as he showed them through to a living room that was decorated with pictures of the planets. Professor Corinth took a seat on a battered-looking leather armchair.

For now, at least, Maya stayed standing. "We needed to ask you about moondials."

"Moondials?" The annoyance in the professor's voice was obvious. "You dragged me out of the shower to talk about *moondials*? Honestly,

I wish I'd never written that book! I was a serious researcher, doing important research that could have pushed forward our understanding of Hawking radiation and the boundaries of black holes by a decade or more. But no, all anyone wants to talk about is moondials. Do you know the number of weirdos and freaks I have to put up with because of that?"

"It's relevant to a case," Maya said. "Tell me, do the names Helene Gretting, Lola Marques, and Aisling Byrne mean anything to you?"

"No," the professor said, and now there was a defensive note in his voice. "Who are they? More young women making unfounded allegations? Is that why you're here?"

"Those three women are dead, Professor Corinth," Maya explained, watching his face to try to read his reaction. He looked shocked, as if it were the last thing he'd been expecting to hear.

"Dead?"

"Where were you last night?" Marco asked, getting the question in while the professor was still off guard.

"I was here all night," Professor Corinth said.

"Alone?" Maya asked.

"Yes, alone."

Meaning that he had no alibi for the most recent murder.

"What about last month? The night of the twenty-seventh?"

The professor looked slightly incredulous at that. "You expect me to remember where I was on a random night… wait, did you say the twenty-seventh?"

"I did," Maya said.

Professor Corinth laughed then.

"What's so funny?" Marco asked.

"Moondials. I said before that they've been the bane of my existence, but this time, I think they've rather saved me. I was giving a talk related to my book out in Wisconsin on the twenty-seventh. It's the kind of thing I have to do these days, since I lost my job. I can give you the names of the organizers, if you need them."

Meaning that he couldn't have been there to kill Lola Marques. Maya had gone off, jumping after the first person connected with moondials that she could find, and the result was that she'd wasted her time.

"I don't even know why you're looking into moondials," the professor said. "Yes, I wrote the book on them, but only as a discussion of the history of science. It's not as if they've ever been considered serious timepieces. They're not even that accurate. Maybe at midnight on the full moon, but every day away from that they lose as much as forty-nine minutes."

"It's not the accuracy that matters," Maya said. "It's the fact that someone is obsessed with them." A thought occurred to her. "Do you know of anyone like that around here? Presumably, someone like that who might get in touch with the biggest expert in the field?"

"Am I supposed to try to identify murderers for you now?" Professor Corinth asked. "No, I can't think of anyone like that. Frankly, I don't have time for such people. Do you know the local astronomy society wanted me to come speak to them without paying me? I'm trying to get back into serious academia. I have no interest in people obsessed with moondials."

"I wish we had that luxury," Maya said. She couldn't help feeling a wave of frustration. She'd thought that they were getting somewhere, but now they had nothing.

She and Marco were going to have to start again.

CHAPTER SIXTEEN

It was dark and he was closing in on his target, following her again, just a little way behind.

Aurora was at a dance class, the same one she attended every week at this time. He sat in his van, watching through the window of the dance studio, watching her move to the rhythm of the beat.

There were plenty of other young women in there with her, many of them as beautiful, as young, as vibrant. In theory, he could have taken any one of them, but that wasn't how he did this. He liked to make plans and follow them precisely.

Precision was important. He measured everything to make sure that it would be exact. He made sure that everything happened at precisely the right time, in precisely the right place. He positioned everything exactly as it should be to produce the perfect moondial, in a beautiful moment of sacrifice to the moon.

He knew, of course, that a moondial wasn't the most precise method of telling the time. If used as simply as a sundial was, then they were anything but accurate, being further and further ahead of the true time the more in front of the full moon one was.

He knew that, and it didn't matter. Not so long as he was precise about the way in which he worked.

The dance class was finishing now, the young women leaving the studio. He ignored all of them except Aurora. Her, he followed, his van creeping along quietly while she got into her car, starting to drive home. He knew where she was going and he knew when he would take her, but he still followed, wanting to leave nothing to chance.

He had the sedative ready. When the moment came, she would be unconscious in seconds, just like the others. Of course, it would be easier to simply stab her, but that wasn't the plan, that wasn't the point. The moment of Aurora's death was as carefully calibrated as her positioning beneath the moon would be, casting the perfect shadow. He wouldn't deviate from that, no matter how much it frustrated him to have to drive along like this behind her, holding back from striking until the perfect moment.

Finally, Aurora reached her home and he drew the van to a halt in front of her building. He slipped out of the van even as she got out of the car. This was the most dangerous moment, the moment where he had the least control over events. Even now, though, he felt confident.

He closed the distance between them swiftly in the dark. Aurora must have heard something, because she started to turn in place to look at him, but he was already on her by the time she was able to do it. One of his hands went across her mouth to stifle any sound, while the other jabbed the syringe home in her flesh, depressing the plunger to send the sedative into her body.

For a moment or two, she tried to scream and fight. He held her close in those moments, stopping her from crying out.

"Shh, it will be over soon," he whispered to her.

He felt the moment when her struggles started to weaken, her strength fading away. He caught her before she could fall to the ground, the sedative working its powerful way through her system. He dragged her then, moving her back to his van.

Not for the first time, he reflected on how easy it would be to simply kill her now, but that wasn't the point of this. That wasn't the way it worked. Yes, a dead body would be easier to transport, but it wouldn't give him that perfect moment when the moon cast exactly the correct shadow. It wouldn't continue the chain of deaths. It would just be random, and he didn't want this to be random.

So he took her into the van, tying her carefully. The moment to kill Aurora would come soon enough. For now, he simply had to wait.

CHAPTER SEVENTEEN

Maya could feel her frustration mounting as she sat back at her borrowed desk with Marco in the Chesterford PD.

"It felt like we were so close to the right idea," Maya said. The lead on the moondials had seemed like the right one to follow, the *only* one to follow. Someone obsessed with the moon seemed like the obvious choice of suspect. Yet the *most* obvious suspect, Professor Corinth, couldn't be the killer. "We went wrong somewhere."

"We're pushing too hard," Marco said.

"Pushing hard is the only choice we have," Maya shot back. "We don't have the time for anything else. We only have a day to solve this."

"But that meant running off after this lead before we'd fully formed it," Marco argued.

He was right, Maya knew that he was right, but that didn't make this any easier. She went to the computer, trying to look for someone else as obsessed with moondials as Professor Corinth had appeared from the outside. Her side ached as she did it, reminding her of the injuries the Moonlight Killer had inflicted on her in their fight. She had to keep going though. She had to, when they only had a day left now.

"This isn't the right way to do this, Maya," Marco said, reaching out for her. Maya shook off his touch.

"It's what I have to do, what *we* have to do," Maya snapped back. "Help me to look for anyone who might be obsessive enough to do this."

"Do you think that will help?" Marco asked. "You already looked for people obsessed with the moon."

"Please, just help me do this," Maya said. She'd been grateful that Marco was there before, because she'd thought that his help was the only assistance she was going to get on this beyond the assistance of the local PD.

"All right," Marco said. "I'll try looking for anyone who might count as moon obsessed, particularly if they have a criminal record, or a record of mental illness. Maybe someone else will show up with a connection to moondials."

That was what Maya was determined to look into. There had to be some connection to them or why would the killer be making them? Marco was right that they'd gone after the professor too quickly, when there could be other people with the same interests, other connections to moondials out there.

She started with Professor Corinth's book. He'd mentioned that his work had brought him into contact with "weirdos and freaks" obsessed with his work. Could that obsession tie into the larger obsession with the moon? Could it show her the killer?

Maya didn't know, but she had to try. She didn't have any better options right then.

Maya started to look at the reviews of the professor's book, at comments about it, at anything she could find that people had written on it. She started to note any comments that looked odd, that seemed to be a little too sure of the work's brilliance, or which spoke about moondials as if they held some mystical significance.

There were more comments and reviews like that than Maya could have imagined. Moondials were meant to be just a way of telling the time at night, but there seemed to be a subset of people who thought that they were more than that, who thought that they had some kind of special, almost mystical significance, who thought that the different phases of them meant something.

Every time Maya saw one of those comments, or simply a comment expressing so much admiration or even hatred that it seemed beyond the usual, Maya noted the username. When it was anything she could easily trace back to a real name, she checked that name against the DMV, trying to work out if there was any chance that the individual was in Chesterford.

"Have you thought about what you'll do after all of this?" Marco asked.

Maya looked up. "What do you mean?"

"When we get Megan back, when we catch the Moonlight Killer. What then?"

Was this his way of reassuring her that they *would* get through this? By trying to get Maya to focus on what came next, was he trying to keep her morale up rather than getting stuck in the work of hunting for suspects?

Or was Marco just interested in what would happen because there was a good chance that it would involve him?

"I don't know," Maya admitted. "I suspect that whether I get to keep my job depends on how all this goes. Even then, I guess Harris will put pressure on to try to get rid of me."

"Whatever happens, I'll be there," Marco promised.

That should have made Maya feel better, it *did* make her feel better, in a lot of ways. However, right then, Maya couldn't afford to give Marco her attention. She had to focus on the case. She had to get *him* to focus on the case.

"Have you found anything?" she asked.

Marco shook his head. "No, or at least, nothing that's solid enough for us to go on. Anything here would just be conjecture, so—"

"Then we'll run with conjecture," Maya said. Right then, she would take anything she could get.

Marco looked a little worried. "Maya, that's what we did with Professor Corinth, and look where that got us."

Maya didn't need him to tell her how badly they'd messed up with that. How badly *she'd* messed up. She'd wasted time that they didn't have. And earlier, with the drive out to the next town to bring in Samuel Lawrentine? Maya found herself silently counting up all the moments that they'd spent in the case so far, assessing everything they'd done and thinking about the time they'd wasted.

"We need to be thorough," Marco said. "We need to make sure that any suspect we come up with has enough to tie them to this case."

Maya shook her head. Didn't Marco understand what was at stake here?

"There's no time to be cautious about all this. Not when we only have another day."

"So, what? Do you just want to bring in a bunch of random suspects off the street?"

Maya could hear just how bad an idea Marco thought that was, and ordinarily she would have agreed, but right then, she didn't want him telling her how to conduct this case. She didn't want him telling her to calm down, or back off, or take a breath. She just wanted to find something that would help them to find the killer before the Moonlight Killer's impossible deadline passed.

"Maybe we should," Maya said. She gestured to the office around them. There weren't many detectives in it at this hour, but there were still a few cops around the precinct. "I have a list of potential suspects, and yes, they're long shots, but maybe we should send the local cops to talk to all of them tonight, just to see if one of them cracks. Maybe we should have them talk to every member of the astronomical society to see if they all have alibis, and work from there."

"And if they don't want to talk to us?" Marco asked.

Maya was determined now. "Then we bring them in and *make* them talk to us."

Maya could only see the worry on Marco's face increasing. It was immediately obvious that he didn't like that idea.

"Maya, we can't just arrest a bunch of people at random. You *know* that. We're the FBI. We still have to do this by the rules."

"Those rules could get my sister killed!" Maya said.

"We'll find a way," Marco insisted. "You're overreacting to all of this, Maya. You've solved cases this bad before. If you just take a moment or two to calm down..."

"Don't tell me to calm down!" Maya said. She was on her feet now and she couldn't remember standing up. "Don't pretend like everything's okay! We're running out of time, and I don't have any idea where to get a lead that will find the killer."

"Maya—" Marco began, but Maya wasn't in the mood to listen.

"No, I don't want to hear it, not right now," Maya said. "I need... I need to clear my head."

She headed for the door. She saw Marco start after her, clearly still worried about her, but she waved him away. She didn't want anyone with her right now, not even Marco.

Maya strode out of the Chesterford police station, out into the night air. She took deep breaths, trying to relax, but she couldn't. With every heartbeat, every breath, Maya was aware of the time ticking away. Every second brought her closer to the Moonlight Killer's deadline.

Had he set this up for her to fail?

That question came to Maya again, impossible to shake off. She'd assumed, she'd *trusted,* that the Moonlight Killer would stick to his own rules, but he could do that and still force her to fail if he simply set a short enough deadline.

Was that what he'd done here? The thought that he might have done so sent a wave of terror running through Maya as she walked along the streets of the town, trying to clear her head.

Yet it also didn't seem to make much sense. The Moonlight Killer didn't *have* to play this game with her. He didn't have to send Maya out on some mystery if he wanted her to fail. She had already broken his rules by trying to save her sister. He could have killed Megan at any point, could simply have left her for Maya to find and then disappeared.

If he'd gone to the trouble of doing this, sending her out on this case, then he presumably wanted Maya to succeed. And if he'd only given her one day, then maybe that was because he believed that she could solve it. Maybe he thought that there was enough there for her to work it out.

But what *was* there for Maya to work with? She'd found a couple of promising suspects who'd proved to have alibis. She'd found many more potential suspects who were much less likely to be connected to all of this. Marco was right: they couldn't just bring in all of them and hope that one of them cracked under the pressure, confessing to the crime.

If the Moonlight Killer was serious about wanting her to solve this case by the deadline, then he had to believe that Maya was already in possession of all the facts about the case that she needed.

Maya had her phone with her, which meant that she had the case files with her. She could have gone back to the precinct to do it, but she didn't want to have to talk to Marco about it, not yet, not before she had something concrete.

Maya started to look through the crime scene photographs, looking for anything that might help her. She found her eye drawn to the pictures of the victims there, and the shadows on the ground in those first photographs. The killer had been using his victims to construct moondials, but why did he want to do that? Had it just been because of his obsession, or was there more to it than that?

Another question came back to Maya then. Why had the killer called in anonymous tips to get the cops on the scene? Because he'd wanted them there at a particular time.

He'd wanted them to see the moondials when the shadows were in particular positions.

Why was that? Maya started to look through the files again, checking the pictures of the victims taken when the police had first arrived, checking the times of the shadows and trying to work out what times those shadows represented. It wasn't exactly, because *moondials* weren't exact, and because the pictures of the scenes would only have been taken when the first CSI officers arrived, but…

Maya's breath caught as she saw it. The times the shadows showed were the same as the times when the next tips were called in, when the next woman had died. The killer was providing a clue to the time of the next murder.

Maya looked at the photographs from the Helene Gretting murder.

She started to run back toward the Chesterford PD, because she knew what time the next murder would take place. And… if the Moonlight Killer had given her such a short deadline… he had to believe that it would be tonight.

CHAPTER EIGHTEEN

Maya ran back into the offices of the Chesterford PD, her excitement at what she'd discovered propelling her forward to the desk where Marco sat at the computer. He seemed to be working hard, concentrating as if he were trying to figure something out.

A part of Maya thought that she should hold back, wait for him to finish, especially when the two of them had just argued over the intensity with which Maya was rushing at this case.

She couldn't, though, not when she'd found something this important.

"Marco, I think I have something," she said.

Marco looked up. He seemed a little worried, and, given the way Maya's last few attempts had gone, she could understand that. He probably thought that she'd come up with some random suspect that she wanted them to throw their efforts at.

Was this the same, though? Maya was aware of how tenuous her idea was. She was having to adjust for the time between the tip-off and when the first photographs at the scene been taken, which meant that there was nothing precise about her working. Even so, she felt confident that she was right, that the killer was deliberately signaling to law enforcement when he would strike next, taunting them with their inability to catch him.

"What have you found?" Marco asked.

"It's something in the crime scene photographs. The killer is making moondials, right?"

"Right," Marco replied, but cautiously, as if wondering where Maya was going with this.

"Which tell the time, but why does he need to tell the time?"

Marco frowned at that. "I'd assumed that he was just making them as objects, because he's so obsessed with the moon and its different phases."

"But then why call in the anonymous tips?" Maya argued. She'd worked all of this out, but now that it was time to justify it all to Marco, she found herself worrying that she might not have gotten some part of it right, that he would see a hole in her reasoning that would mean it all fell apart.

No, her reasoning was fine. She was right about this.

Marco seemed to get it then. "Because he wants the police there at a particular time."

"Now look at the reports from the coroner," Maya said. "None of the bodies were fresh when the police got there. The victims had been tied in place, killed, and then left, with the killer only calling in the tip afterwards."

That was important, otherwise it would simply mean the murderer taking the life of a young woman at the same time each time he struck. By killing his victims first and only then calling in the tip, he created a puzzle for the police to solve; one that Maya believed that she *had* solved.

"So you're saying that by calling the tip in, he wanted the police to see the moondial at a particular time, and that time corresponds to the time when he's going to kill his next victim?" Marco said.

"Exactly." Maya was glad that he'd gotten that part. "And if we look at the photographs from the last crime scene…"

Maya pulled them up for Marco to see. The shadow of the moon was clearly visible.

"This first photograph was taken by Officer Sorenson shortly after he arrived at the scene," Maya said. "It's the closest thing we have to the time the killer wants to show."

"That's in less than an hour, assuming that the killer is planning to strike again tonight."

"My guess is that he will. Or at least, that the Moonlight Killer thinks that he will."

She saw Marco's eyes widen slightly. "Because why give you the short deadline otherwise? But what has he spotted that we haven't?"

"Maybe he worked out the killer's identity another way," Maya said. "Maybe this is someone who is only in town occasionally, which explains why he only kills here sometimes. Maybe it has something to do with the phases of the moon. You can bet that the Moonlight Killer would spot something like *that*."

"The phases of the moon!" Marco said, obviously excited. "I was going to tell you, I came up with something too. I think there's a pattern to the locations of the murders."

That caught Maya by surprise. "All I was able to see was a vague kind of arc to them."

"A very *deliberate* arc," Marco said. He gestured to his computer screen. "Look."

He'd plotted out the locations of the murders on the map, along with a line joining them together. It was a smooth arc, with no obvious deviation. The killer had been precise about where he'd chosen to kill his victims.

"I think that each of the spots corresponds to the position of the moon in the night sky," Marco said. "The killer is trying to achieve a very specific effect."

That realization made all of this work. It potentially gave them both a time and a place where the next murder was going to happen. If they could just work out that location…

"Have you been able to find out where the next murder will take place?" Maya asked.

"I'm waiting for a call," Marco said.

"Not from our techs?" Maya said, sudden worry running through her. The Moonlight Killer had been very clear about not using FBI help on this.

"No, I realized that we had access to an expert right here in Chesterford."

Almost as he said it, his phone started to ring. Marco took it and put it on speaker.

"Professor Corinth, thank you for getting back to me so quickly."

"Do you know what time it is, Detective?" the professor demanded with obvious bad grace.

"I do, sir, probably better than you, right now. By my colleague's reckoning, we have less than an hour to save the life of a young woman. Now, have you had a chance to look at the map I sent you?"

"Briefly."

"Based on the phases of the moon, is it possible to plot the next location in the sequence on the map?"

"Well, yes, it's a rather simple mathematical exercise, based on the apparent positioning of the moon in the night sky. There is more shift from night to night than most people think, and this model seems to amplify that shift, but… yes, I believe I have it." He made it sound easy to work out, rather than something that would have left anyone else confused, unable to come up with an answer.

"And where is the next location?" Marco asked.

"I've sent the map back to you with it marked. While I hope that this helps, I hope you'll also understand that I would prefer you not to contact me again."

Maya would be just as happy not hearing from the professor again, although she suspected that when this went to court, he might find himself called as a witness now.

When, not if. For almost the first time in this case, it felt like they were close to finding real answers. Maya looked at the version of the map the professor had sent across. A point was marked there clearly, continuing the arcing line across the city. There was a note to one side about the mathematics he'd used to predict the positioning, but to Maya, the most important thing was that it looked right. It looked like the kind of place where it might be possible for the killer to do something like this: a large open space in the middle of an industrial area. At this time of the night, with most of the businesses there closed, the killer would have a free shot to position his victim and kill her.

"We have the time and the place," Maya said. "We need to get over there now."

"And the local PD?" Marco asked. "We can surround the area, get them to converge on him once he's in place."

Maya shook her head to that. She'd had too many bad experiences with Harris's raids to trust that something like that would go well.

"There's too much of a risk that he sees that something's wrong. Especially with so little time to plan all of this. If he sees that the police are there, he might abandon his plans, and we might never catch him. Certainly not before the deadline."

Marco looked a little doubtful. "We should at least have some backup in place. What if he runs?"

"We'll call for backup once we have eyes on him," Maya said. "And if he runs, we chase him. It needs to be the two of us, Marco. Any more than that and we risk losing everything."

*

Maya sat in the remains of an abandoned warehouse, looking out at the spot the professor had indicated for them on the map. Around her, a series of industrial presses sat unused, abandoned where they were whenever the business that had been here had folded.

She kept low, doing her best to avoid any sign that she was there as she kept watch. They couldn't afford any chance that the killer would spot them there.

Marco was a little way from her, looking out another window. It was important to cover as many lines of approach as they could. He looked serious and brooding, ready for anything that the night threw at him. Maya was glad to have him on her side in this.

The space beyond the warehouse seemed perfect for what the killer wanted. It was large and open, with plenty of room for the moonlight above to shine down. It was close enough to the rest of the town that the police could be there quickly in response to the tip-off when it came. It was silent now, with no sign of people around. Even if someone saw the killer pull up with a strange-looking contraption, if they didn't see the body of his victim immediately, then they might simply assume that he was bringing something to one of the businesses there after hours.

Maya was ready for trouble, wearing a tactical vest, with her Glock waiting in its holster. She had decided against a longer rifle for tonight, because there was a good chance that they would be dealing with the killer at close quarters, potentially while he had a hostage. She shifted the vest slightly, trying to relieve some of the discomfort of it rubbing against her injuries.

That thought immediately took Maya back to the moment when she'd confronted the Moonlight Killer in his bunker, when he'd taken Megan as a hostage, destroying the bunker so that he could escape. If Maya had been able to find a clean shot then, none of this would have happened.

If she got the chance to take the killer down tonight, she wouldn't hesitate. Just as she wouldn't hesitate the next time she faced the Moonlight Killer.

Maya checked her watch. They were approaching the time for the killer to arrive according to the moondials, yet she couldn't see any sign of him from her vantage point.

Maya moved over to Marco in a low crouch, not wanting to risk the slightest flicker of movement being seen through the windows of the abandoned building where they waited.

"Any sign of movement?" Maya asked.

Marco shook his head. "All quiet. The last thing that came through was that truck fifteen minutes ago."

That worried Maya. They'd been there for a while now, with no sign of the killer approaching and the time for the murder coming up quickly. If they'd gotten this wrong, if they were in the wrong spot, then they might miss their chance to catch the killer somewhere else. He might already be there, moving his victim into position.

“He’ll show,” Marco said, obviously understanding what she was thinking. “The pattern is clear, and this… well, you can see it’s the right spot.”

Maya nodded. This was indeed the perfect spot, but that only made it stranger that the killer wasn’t there. She checked her watch. They only had a couple of minutes until the time that the last moondial had shown. Even if the reading hadn’t been accurate, there should have been some sign of the killer by now.

“I’m going to change position,” Maya said. “Maybe we just aren’t seeing something from this angle. The professor’s calculations can only have been so precise.”

Without waiting for an answer, she started toward the door to the warehouse. Even as she did so, however, something caught Maya’s attention out of the corner of her eye. She froze in place instinctively, looking out through the nearest window.

There was movement there. The killer was here.

CHAPTER NINETEEN

Maya signaled to Marco, getting him to move over to her to see what was happening. She winced at every small sound he made as he crossed the space to the window, even though she knew that it was unlikely that the killer would be able to hear either of them at this distance.

"He's here," Maya whispered, so quietly that it was barely more than a breath. "One o'clock."

There was movement there near one of the other buildings, faint enough that it would be easy for Maya to dismiss it as a figment of her imagination if it weren't for the fact that she'd been trained in this kind of waiting and watching, both by the FBI and by military intelligence before that. She knew how to look over an area systematically, how to watch for potential threats, and how to recognize them when they *did* appear.

She'd also learned the difference between the natural movements of animals and the environment around her, and the kind of movement that suggested someone trying to be stealthy.

The movement came again, a flash of someone running between one building and another.

"I see him," Marco whispered back. Maya could hear the tension in his voice. He was obviously ready for action, ready for the possibility that the killer would try to kill either them or the woman he had tied in place to be his victim.

Maya put a hand on his arm, signaling for him to wait. They needed the killer to come closer, where the two of them could take him down more easily.

A figure moved out into the open space beyond the buildings, moving furtively, looking around carefully as if checking for anyone watching. Did he know that Maya and Marco were there? No, Maya didn't think so. He wasn't looking their way, just looking in every direction, obviously making sure that he was alone.

It was hard to make out much about him. He seemed to be a little over average height, but he was wearing a long, dark coat that obscured much of his form, with a hood up over his face to disguise his features.

He was wearing gloves. All of it contributed to Maya's feeling that this was someone here to do something criminal. This had to be their guy.

The slightly worrying part was that he *was* alone. He didn't have the mechanism of the moondial with him, or the victim he was going to kill.

"Do we wait for him to bring out the victim?" Marco asked, echoing Maya's thoughts.

Maya considered that. Doing so would make it easy to prove this man's connection to the crimes, so it made a lot of sense to wait. At the same time, though, they had no way of knowing whether he would take the opportunity to kill his victim if they let him get out of sight. There could be a woman tied up and drugged somewhere who might die if Maya and Marco gave this man any chance to return to her.

"I don't think that we can risk it," Maya said. "If his victim is still alive, then we can't risk letting him go back to her. There's too much of a chance that he kills her that way. We have to take him down now."

Marco nodded. "All right. Give me ten seconds to move to the far door. That way, we can hit him from both sides."

It was a good idea. Coming at the suspect from multiple angles would give him less of a chance to escape. Maya moved to her own exit and started counting silently.

She'd made it to eight when Marco swung open the other door to the abandoned warehouse and Maya realized the flaw in their plan. It was clearly a door that hadn't been opened in a long time, which meant that it was one that rattled and creaked as Marco opened it.

Maya saw the figure start at the sound, looking around in the direction of the warehouse. The moment she saw that, she knew there was no more time to spend waiting and watching. She had to act.

Maya hurried forward out the door, drawing her Glock as she went and leveling it at her suspect. This was a dangerous man and, judging by the knife wounds on the victims, almost certainly armed.

"FBI, freeze! Put your hands in the air!"

It should have worked, should have been enough to gain compliance from her suspect. Instead, though, he turned and bolted, heading for the cluster of buildings around the open space.

Maya cursed, because she couldn't just fire on a fleeing suspect, couldn't just shoot at an unarmed man. Instead, she set off in pursuit, sprinting after him, determined to bring him down.

"Marco, he's running!" she called out.

Maya followed the fleeing figure, doing her best to ignore the pain of the still healing wound in her side as she did so, even though it burned like fire as she ran. It meant that Maya wasn't as fast as she normally would have been. On any other day, she might have run down the suspect in seconds, tackling him and cuffing him almost as soon as they hit the ground.

Instead, the two of them raced on between the warehouses and the factories of the industrial area.

They ran down an alley between two factories, with dumpsters down the sides and abandoned pieces of metalwork propped up against the outside walls. The fleeing killer grabbed one of the dumpsters, swinging it out into Maya's path.

Maya dodged around it as best she could, but it cost her a couple of seconds, and those seconds were all her suspect needed to open up the gap between them again. Maya ran on, hoping that the fleeing figure would run out of breath soon, because the pain from the wound the Moonlight Killer had inflicted on her was only growing.

Her suspect darted out of sight around a corner and, for a moment or two at least, Maya lost track of him. She hurried to the corner, but she still had to take it slowly, checking the angles to make sure he wasn't going to leap out at her as she rounded it.

That hesitation cost her, because by the time Maya got around the corner, the suspect had disappeared. Maya quickly glanced around herself, trying to make sure that the suspect wasn't about to leap out at her from some hidden corner. That was when she saw the door to one of the factories hanging open.

Maya pushed her way inside, pulling out a flashlight and using its beam to light up the machinery ahead of her. This seemed to be some kind of textile factory, with massive looms and spinning machines taking up most of the space. Maya moved forward cautiously, picking her way between the machinery, trying not to get snagged on any errant pieces of cloth.

Around her, the place was eerily still and silent, the only sound Maya's breathing as she kept going forward. Her side ached, the wound there painful, but there was nothing she could do about it. She could take the time to go to an emergency room to get checked out once all of this was over. First, she had to catch a killer.

Then, she had to get her sister back.

There was a patch of moonlight shining in through a large skylight above. Maya realized that it was enough to see by without the flashlight, so she turned it off and crept forward through the dark. In a situation like this, it was better not to let the suspect see where she was.

Maya thought she heard a sound somewhere behind her: the scrape of a boot on the concrete floor. Maya advanced toward it, moving quietly. There was a figure there, barely visible in the half-dark.

Maya leapt out, gun leveled again. "Freeze! Hands in the air, right now!"

The figure raised his hands and it was only then that Maya realized her mistake.

"Maya, it's me," Marco said, stepping out more into the light.

Of course he would have been only a few paces behind her, following as she chased down her suspect. Marco wouldn't just abandon her to take on a dangerous killer alone.

Maya lowered her weapon. "He's in here somewhere. We need to search. Stay together."

In the dark, if they split up, there was too much of a chance of bumping into one another again. If one of them reacted by firing… no, it was far better to stick together. It meant that they could cover one another as they searched.

Maya stalked through the near dark, leading the way, trying to concentrate on her senses, pushing them to their limits. It was slow going. They had to pause at the edge of every piece of machinery, checking around its corners to make sure that their suspect wasn't there.

Then Maya heard a sound, away to her left. She hurried toward it with Marco in her wake. The sound had come from among some large containers of folded linen, huge tubs of it like the world's largest laundry baskets. Maya thought she saw a figure slipping between two of them.

That was when he pushed one of the baskets, tipping its contents toward Maya and Marco. Linen poured out of it in a wave that was almost enough to knock Maya from her feet, covering her and overwhelming her. In that moment, she was blind, thrashing around wildly in an attempt to break free of the grip of the cloth as it threatened to smother her.

That was when she heard the sound of running footsteps next to her. Even caught up in the cloth as she was, Maya reached out toward the sound automatically. She felt her hand latch onto a leg and she yanked, bearing her suspect to the floor.

He fought then, and as Maya broke free of the grip of the linen, she could see the gleam of a knife in his hand. Maya grabbed for that hand, and realized that she had something even better than just trying to hold on. She whipped the linen next to her around that limb, swaddling it and the knife, covering it so thickly that the weapon couldn't do anything.

Marco was there then, helping her to roll their suspect over onto his stomach in the dark. He was thrashing wildly, so that it took both of their efforts, but they finally managed to get his hands behind his back and cuff him. Maya knelt there for several seconds, barely able to get the breath back to say the next part.

"You're under arrest."

CHAPTER TWENTY

"Tea, Megan?"

The most terrifying part for Megan was how normal her captor was being, even now. How polite, how friendly. This was a man who had kidnapped her and twelve other women, who had hurt her, who had killed at least one of those women. This was a man she was sure was planning to kill her.

"Would you like tea?" he repeated.

They were sitting in the kitchen of an old farmhouse. It looked comfortable, even cozy, except that Megan's arms were tied to the chair she was sitting on, leaving her helpless.

"I'd rather know your name," she said. "I've seen your face now, so I figure that you don't care anymore about me knowing who you are. You might as well tell me your name."

Megan knew she should have felt terror in that moment, at the possible reasons he might have let her see his face. Megan was sure now that he planned to kill her at some point; he was simply waiting. Yet she seemed to have moved beyond terror, into a kind of determined space where she was strangely calm. If he gave her any opportunity to get out of there, she would take it.

"People call me Frank," he said. "I had another name once, but Frank is what I've been called ever since the military."

"You were in the military?" Megan said. That didn't surprise her. She'd seen the way he'd used weapons smoothly, efficiently. Then there was the fact that he'd rigged his whole bunker to explode.

"I was." There was a faint note of pain there, as if something had happened to him, deep in the past. Megan knew she had to ask. At this point, she couldn't *not* know.

"What happened there?"

Frank smiled then. "Do you really want to know me, or is this some attempt to try to get closer to me so that I'll hesitate when it comes to killing you, Megan?"

Megan stared at him levelly, not wanting to back down now.

"I know you won't hesitate with me, or anyone," she said. "I know you're a psychopath."

That made a brief flicker of anger cross Frank's face.

"That's an ugly word, used by fools. They were happy enough in the army when I crept in at night, under the moon, killing my targets. Yet somehow the same thing is evil when I do it for myself? Do you want to know about the most important night of my life, Megan?"

Megan nodded, because Frank's tone of voice made it sound as if she didn't have a choice.

"I was with my unit. Twelve others in total. We were infiltrating a base in… well, I won't bore you with the details. One conflict fades into another after a while. Suffice it to say that every one of those men died around me, killed by the enemy. But I survived. I escaped. And I found myself thinking why. Why did I survive?"

Megan frowned at that. She couldn't imagine a man like this suffering any kind of survivor's guilt.

"I decided that it was because I was superior to all of them," Frank said after a second or two. "Since then, twelve has been a special number for me. The moon has been special for me. With this cycle, the idea was to show myself superior to twelve of those whose petty murders muddied the waters of my own work. Twelve would-be greatest killers, there to take my crown. I've killed some of them, you know?"

Megan shook her head. "So, when you were away from the bunker…"

"Oh, not all of it was killing my rivals. Some of them, I had killed instead. A couple, I just left to rot. Twelve, it was meant to be twelve. And of course, along the way, a contest with an opponent who might actually be worthy of the name."

"My sister," Megan guessed.

Frank smiled at that. "Indeed. Your sister. Which is why I don't mind telling you all of this, of course."

"Because you're planning to kill her, and me," Megan said. "You're planning to use me to lure her in. I won't let you do that. I won't be a part of it!"

Frank reached out to touch her face. Then his grip tightened painfully on her jaw.

"You won't have a choice. And neither will she. That's the best kind of plan: when someone knows what is happening but it happens anyway. Tonight, either your sister will defeat me, or both you and she will die. And Megan… there is no way for her to beat me."

CHAPTER TWENTY ONE

Maya sat in the interrogation room of the Chesterford PD, wondering if she was sitting across from a killer. He was thin faced and pockmarked, with dark, lank hair and dark eyes so deep-set that they looked almost hollow. Was this what Maya had imagined when she thought of the murderer?

The public defender was there, looking harassed at having to be there so late. He looked almost too young to be a lawyer, short and blond, wearing a cheap suit and a shirt that clearly hadn't been pressed in a while.

Marco, meanwhile, was standing near the far wall, looking on and clearly hiding whatever pain he felt from his still healing bullet wound in the aftermath of the arrest. Maya certainly was, pushing down her pain so that she could focus on her job.

Local PD hadn't managed to find a body, or a captive, yet. She needed to get something here. She needed evidence. She needed a confession.

"So, let's start with the basics of who you are," Maya said. She pushed a sheet of paper across the metal table that lay between her and the men opposite her. "We ran your prints. You're Neil Cooper, of no known address, and you have a rap sheet a mile long. What were you doing in the industrial area, Neil?"

The lawyer started to speak. "My client won't be saying—"

"Maybe I was just out for an evening stroll," Neil said, before the lawyer could finish. Maya was grateful for that. He was a talker. It was always easier to interrogate someone when they were at least prepared to engage.

"A stroll in which you just happened to go to the spot where we believe a killer was about to murder his next victim, while carrying a knife?" Marco interjected.

Cooper didn't react. It was hard to tell whether that was because he was a hardened criminal who had been in this position too many times before, because he was a psychopath who simply wasn't affected by it all, or both.

"I like to go walking in abandoned areas," Cooper said. "It's peaceful."

"And you just *happened* to walk up at the exact moment we were expecting a killer, in the exact place we were expecting him?" Maya asked.

The lawyer cut in. "That's circumstantial at best, Agent. My client happens to walk in the wrong place and so you've arrested him?"

"We've arrested him for the part where he tried to stab me," Maya shot back. She wasn't about to let the lawyer take control of the interrogation. If he got his way, Cooper wouldn't say anything and then they would be left trying to find some shred of physical proof to tie him to the murders. Maya didn't want to have to hope that they would find that in time, before the Moonlight Killer's deadline ran out.

"That was self-defense," Cooper said. "Two figures tried to attack me without identifying themselves. I was only trying to protect myself."

Maya had identified herself as FBI when she'd first confronted him, so she knew that Cooper was simply lying, playing games because he could. The risk was that he would be able to spin those games out past the deadline. She couldn't allow that.

"Tell me about moondials, Neil," she said.

He shrugged. "I don't know anything about that. What is it, like a sundial or something?"

He made it sound so innocent, like he didn't know anything.

"Let's ask a different question then," Marco said. "Where's the woman you were planning to kill?"

Cooper raised an eyebrow and shrugged. "What woman? I don't know anything about any woman."

He sounded so plausible, so believable, yet Maya got the feeling that he would sound exactly the same way, no matter what lie he chose to tell. She sat there, looking over his police record for a moment or two. He'd been arrested multiple times for drunken fights, for theft, for drugs. Was this what he did when he was arrested, spinning out lies and denials in the hope that law enforcement didn't have anything on him? Were those violent tendencies a sign of something more? Were they an indication of a building darkness that had spilled over into murder?

"When did you get into town?" Maya asked.

Cooper shrugged. "I don't know. I come and go."

"If I were to give you dates, would you be able to tell me whether you were in town or not?" Maya asked.

That just got another shrug. That shrug raised Maya's hopes, because it meant that he had no alibi. There was nothing to say that he couldn't have killed the three victims to date.

At the same time, though, it made things complicated. He wasn't lying in a way that would be easy to check and disprove. It didn't give Maya and Marco anything to latch onto. They would need physical evidence to tie him to the crime.

Marco seemed determined to keep up the pressure, hoping that Cooper would crack. "As we're speaking, forensics are checking the knife that you tried to kill us with to see if it's a match for the wounds on the victims. We're also using traffic cam footage to look for a black panel van that the DMV says is registered to you. We'll find it, which means that we'll find the victim you were planning to kill there. At that point, this is done. If you want to make things easier on yourself, talk now."

Cooper stared back blankly. "I don't know anything about any of that, and if you find my van… well, good luck finding it, but *if* you find it, it will be empty."

Maya sat there staring at him, trying to think of a way to get to the answers that she needed. She could also feel worry starting to build up inside her. She couldn't help checking her watch. They only had a little over forty-five minutes until midnight. Less than an hour before her sister died at the Moonlight Killer's hands.

"Got somewhere you need to be?" Cooper asked casually, as if he weren't in a world of trouble.

Maya stood up, walking out of the room, gesturing for Marco to follow her. He came out with her, the two of them standing outside the interrogation room, looking into it through a one-way mirror at Cooper and his lawyer. Cooper looked far too relaxed in there.

"What if it's not him?" Maya asked, unable to keep her fears for her sister out of her voice.

"He was in the right place at the right time. He tried to kill you when we went to arrest him. And he's obviously a criminal."

"Obviously a criminal, yes," Maya said. "But is he the killer?"

"We can't just let him go and start again," Marco pointed out. "Our best shot is to keep going and try to get a confession from him. He's confident now, but we can use that against him if we keep him talking."

Maya wasn't so sure about that. She certainly wasn't sure if they could do it in time. She needed to think. She needed to work out what their options were, to try to find a way to connect him to the crime, or to work out, if he wasn't the killer, where she and Marco had gone wrong.

"Keep going in there," Maya said to him. "I need to think."

Marco nodded. "I'll get him to talk. I know how much time pressure we're under. Have you thought about how the Moonlight Killer will know that you've succeeded?"

"My guess is that he'll still monitor open police channels," Maya said. "So I'll announce it over that. It's the best option we have."

First, though, she needed to be sure that they'd arrested the right guy. Maya headed back through to the desk she'd borrowed, sitting down and trying to think.

What worried her was that they hadn't caught Neil Cooper with his victim. If, from what Maya had seen in the crime scene reports and the coroner's notes, the killer took his victims to the locations where he was going to kill them, he secured them in place and then he killed them at the appointed time. Shouldn't Cooper have had a victim with him, in that case? Shouldn't he have been setting up the frame that he would use to hold her?

It was possible that Maya and Marco had simply interrupted him before he could finish his grisly work, but, if so, why had his van been parked somewhere obvious nearby? Was it possible that the victim was still there, waiting for them to find her?

If so, why was Cooper so confident that his van would be found empty? Was that just a bluff? Was all of his calmness in there just to try to deflect them from really looking into him? Was he so much of a psychopath that he simply didn't feel the fear or worry that should have been overwhelming him in that moment?

Maya certainly felt it all.

They should have found the victim. They should have found the frame, but at the same time, he'd been in the right place at the right time. He'd been the *only* person in that place at that time. Didn't that *have* to make him the killer?

What was the alternative? That his presence in the industrial area had scared off the killer? That the killer had somehow spotted Maya and Marco moving into position and decided to abandon his plans?

Maya wasn't sure that she believed either of those possibilities. This was a killer who was precise about what he did, who seemed to be acting out some elaborate ritual of his own devising, taking people and turning them into nothing more than devices for telling the time.

So what else did that leave? Had she and Marco made a mistake? Had Professor Corinth gotten the location wrong?

Maya doubted that. The man clearly knew what he was doing. For the same reason, she didn't doubt that the Moonlight Killer had given her this deadline for a reason.

She must have made a mistake somewhere though or…

Wait, what had Professor Corinth said about moondials? That they were inaccurate. That they only told the correct time on the night of the full moon. Every day before that, they were up to forty-nine minutes fast. Which meant that tonight, two nights before the full moon…

Maya practically leapt out of her seat. The professor had done calculations on the location for them, but Maya had been the one to work out the time. They'd been in the right place, but ninety-eight minutes too early. The killer was still out there, getting ready to kill his victim even now.

At least, Maya thought that he was. She had to check, and that meant going back to the industrial area. Either she would find a different killer there now, or she would find Neil Cooper's van and his victim. Maybe he'd gone there to scout the ground before he struck. She would have an answer either way.

Yet she didn't call for Marco to accompany her. Maya knew that with so little time, she couldn't bet everything on one theory, one realization. He had to stay here to keep working to get a confession from Cooper. If he was the killer, then they needed something solid to prove it before the deadline.

Marco needed to be here, continuing the interrogation, but Maya… Maya needed to get back to the spot where they'd calculated that the killer would strike, before it was too late.

CHAPTER TWENTY TWO

Carl drove with Aurora in the trunk of his car, heading for the location where her life would end. A life that had started on the wrong day, at the wrong time. He needed her to keep the cycle going.

Carl could see the moon up above, two days from full, gibbous already and waxing further. The same phase of the moon that Aurora had been born in, at night in the local hospital.

Carl knew that, just as he knew the birth dates and times of the others he'd killed. Each of them had been born under a different phase of the moon. Each of them had died at the time the next of his victims had been born, following the waxing and waning of the moon, building through its endless cycle.

Carl had been fascinated by the moon since was a child, when his parents had decided that his behavior was too "dangerous," too "wrong." His mother had wanted to take him to see a doctor after he'd killed the first animals, but his father had known best. His father had *always* known best.

"Beating the badness out of him is the only way," he'd said. So he'd beaten Carl with his hands, or his belt, then locked Carl away in his room like a prisoner, like an animal.

Carl had nothing in that room except for a few schoolbooks and whatever food his parents saw fit to give him. He hadn't even had a clock to judge the passage of time, a calendar to mark the shifting days.

All he'd had was the moon looking down at him, showing Carl the love that his parents never did. The moon didn't judge Carl for what he was, what he did. Instead, she encouraged him, whispering to him, helping him to become the man he was today. He could hear her now, demanding blood, demanding the sacrifice that was rightfully hers.

Carl had learned a lot from the moon. He'd learned how to shift the way he appeared to others, how to reflect back at them what they wanted to see. He'd learned that things had their natural patterns of growth and life… and ending.

He'd learned how to pretend to be the son his parents wanted, how to become a straight-A student, how to fit in. He'd gotten a job at the records office in the town where he'd lived. Then, a few months ago, he'd heard that his parents had died, back in Chesterford. He'd moved home, and the moon had started whispering to him again.

He'd joined the local astronomical society and the whispers had become more insistent. He'd heard about the astronomer who'd moved here, Professor Corinth, which had led to his book on moondials.

Then, the whispers had become a roar.

He'd listened, and finally, killing had been the most liberating experience of his life. He'd transformed the way the moon transformed, finally becoming the man he was meant to be. He should have done it years ago, but he'd always thought that with his parents alive, they would somehow know, so he'd held back, only hurt people a little, been cruel in small ways.

Now, he didn't need to hold back. He could give the moon her due.

"Soon," he promised her, continuing to drive. "We'll be there at the right time. You'll get your sacrifice soon."

CHAPTER TWENTY THREE

Maya raced back to the industrial area, hoping that she would be in time, pushing her car to the limits to get there. She skidded around a corner, barely slowing down enough to make it, then kept going. There wasn't much time left, even according to her new calculation.

Worse, midnight was approaching fast. If that came and went, it didn't *matter* if she caught the killer or not. Her sister would still be dead. The Moonlight Killer would still take the excuse to strangle her.

Maya couldn't allow that to happen. She pulled the car into the industrial area at speed, brakes complaining as she drew to a halt and all but leapt from the car. Maya knew that she didn't have any time to simply sit and watch, the way she had before. She had to hunt more actively for any sign of a vehicle that the killer might be using. If that meant that she found Neil Cooper's van and a victim within, that would still be a result. If it meant that she found a different killer, then that would prove her latest theory right and she would be in position to take him down.

Maya started to make her way through the industrial area, looking for any sign of anything out of place. The moon shone above through the gaps between the buildings, lending a silvery light to everything around Maya.

By it, she expected to see a killer, expected to spot at least a vehicle that might be Neil Cooper's. Yet, as Maya made her way around the spaces between the factories and the warehouses, she couldn't see any sign of life there. Maya started to circle back around toward the open space at the heart of it all, to the spot where she was so certain the killer would be.

He was rapidly running out of time to get there. Did that mean that he wasn't coming? Had Maya miscalculated again? Had she made another mistake, one that would prove fatal for Megan this time? The thought of that was terrifying.

Maya had to be right about this, yet the longer she waited, the less likely it seemed that she was. Maybe Neil Cooper was the killer after all? Or maybe it was someone else but they simply weren't planning to strike again tonight. Maybe they were leaving it until next month, or the month after that, long after the Moonlight Killer's deadline.

Maya was so caught up in her thoughts that she jumped when her phone buzzed, alerting her to a text. It was from Marco.

Where are you? Cooper still isn't saying anything about murders, but is admitting to being there looking to steal from the factories. Not sure if he's the killer. Holding him anyway for attacking us.

Maya considered her options. Should she tell Marco to keep going with what he was doing and not say anything more? Or should she tell him about the idea she'd had and risk pulling him away from an interrogation that might still crack the case?

I went back to the industrial area, she sent back. *My calculations on the time were off by 98 minutes. I think the killer should only be arriving now.*

The killer should be here. The adjusted calculation said as much. If Maya's theory was right, if he really was killing his victims at the time that the moondial indicated, then he should be here.

He wasn't, though. There was no sign of anyone. Maybe Maya should turn around and head back to the Chesterford PD. Maybe she should rejoin Marco and try to get a confession out of Neil Cooper before the deadline, whatever it took.

Even as Maya decided that she would turn back, she found herself back on the fringes of the open space between the warehouses—and there, in the middle of it all, was the killer.

Not just the killer. This time, there could be no doubt that it was him, because a large metal and wood frame was already in place there at what appeared to be a carefully calculated spot on the ground.

He was a tall man, his face obscured by a mask, his dark hair spilling down to shoulder length. He was wearing a dark jacket and jeans, while his hands were covered by gloves. He'd obviously taken precautions to make sure that he didn't leave any physical evidence behind at the scene, and that caution said a lot about why they hadn't been able to find anything to link him to the murders.

A car stood just a little way away, dented and old, nondescript and cheap. Even as Maya watched, the killer started back toward it, heading for the trunk.

Maya wondered then if she should call for backup to help take the killer down. Should she call Marco to let him know that she'd located the killer? Maya wanted to do so, but she wasn't sure that there was any time in which to do it. Maya couldn't afford the extra noise, either, not against the near silence of the industrial area.

She crept forward instead, trying to close the distance between herself and the killer, trying to get into a position where she could safely apprehend the killer. Maya drew her gun as she moved forward, knowing that this killer would be too dangerous to take down hand to hand.

Even as Maya started to close the distance, she saw the killer open the trunk of the car, dragging a young woman from it as if she were little more than dead weight. Was she dead already? That wasn't how this was meant to work. No, she had to be alive. He'd tied her up, after all. Why do that if she were already dead? Maya had no way of knowing if her guess was true or not, but she had to hope, had to believe that she still had a chance to save this young woman's life.

Maya saw the killer start toward the shape of the moondial, dragging his victim as he went. Maya knew she was still too far away to take the killer down, but she was running out of time. The killer was there, advancing on the moondial, and once he reached it, once he got his victim into position, he would kill her. Maybe he would take his time before he did that, but maybe he would do it immediately, giving Maya no time in which to act.

Maya kept trying to close the distance. It wasn't far now. Yet trying to move silently meant that there were limits to how quickly she could move. The time it was taking to close the gap gave the killer all the time he needed to start to strap his victim into position on the moondial. Maya knew she couldn't allow him to finish that.

She was out of time. Maya ran forward now, not caring how much noise her feet made as they clattered on the concrete. The noise meant that the killer looked around toward her, the suddenness of the movement betraying his shock that she was there.

A knife flashed in the moonlight and Maya knew she had no more time in which to keep closing the distance. She had to act.

"FBI! Drop your weapon!"

The killer ducked back behind his victim and Maya fired, but the shot went wide. With a hostage in the way, at this distance, it was hard to get a clean shot. The sound of the gunshot filled the emptiness of the night, overwhelmingly loud.

The noise and the threat of it was enough to startle the killer into motion. Maya had been worried that he would kill his victim then and there, but he bolted instead, heading for his car.

This time, Maya didn't have to worry about whether her shot was clear. She fired twice, hitting her target both times. The two tires of the car closest to her burst as Maya shot them, shredding and deflating, taking away the killer's chance to use the vehicle to escape.

"Put your hands up!" Maya called out. "Drop the weapon!"

He did neither of those things. Instead, he ran again, this time heading for the maze of alleys among the buildings.

Maya had an instant in which to make a decision, an instant in which to decide whether to shoot. This was an armed killer, but he wasn't posing an immediate threat now, merely trying to get away. Cursing to herself, Maya set off in pursuit, trying to keep up.

The running immediately made her side hurt where she'd been shot by the Moonlight Killer, the pain of it sharp and immediate. It meant that the killer was able to pull ahead of her, and a small part of Maya told her that she should stop, that she should give up. Maya ignored that part. She couldn't give up now. She only had a few more minutes before midnight, a few more minutes before time ran out for her sister. She *had* to catch up to the killer.

Maya ran on, following her suspect through the twists and turns of the industrial area. She had the advantage now that she had already chased Neil Cooper this way, so she already knew where the obstacles were, letting Maya dodge around them without any trouble. That meant that she was able to keep pace with the killer, but even so, when he ducked out of sight around a corner, Maya lost sight of him for a second or two.

Maya followed at speed, with no time to be cautious. Even so, by the time she got around the corner, there was no sign of the killer.

Maya's first instinct was to check the doors of nearby buildings, in case he had ducked inside one the way Cooper had. Those all seemed to be closed, though, leaving Maya standing there, heart hammering, wondering where the killer had gone.

It was only then that Maya spotted the ladder leading up one side of the building she was next to. Maya looked up then and saw the killer just cresting the roof, disappearing from sight once again.

Ignoring the pain in her side, Maya hurried to the ladder and started to climb.

CHAPTER TWENTY FOUR

Maya pulled herself up onto the rooftop, rolling onto it, bringing up her weapon in case the killer took the opportunity to attack. She felt ready for action in that moment, but also terrified by the passing seconds. It wasn't long until midnight now. She had to catch him.

The killer wasn't coming after her, though, but running, his silhouette visible against the light of the moon. Maya got to her feet, wincing at the pain of it. She started to run, trying to close the distance between them. The killer was running across the rooftop, dodging between ventilation outlets and chimneys.

Maya saw him look back, his mask a sudden flash of paleness against the dark. For a moment, Maya thought he might turn and fight, but at this distance, with her gun against his knife, Maya was the one with the advantage.

Maybe that was why he *didn't* turn to fight, but instead ran for the edge of the roof. Maya saw him reach it, and she couldn't help a gasp as he leapt out into space.

Had he flung himself off the building to escape capture? Had he killed himself so that Maya wouldn't be able to bring him in? Maya ran up to the edge of the roof, forcing herself to look down, afraid of what she would see when she did.

What she saw wasn't a body on the ground below, though, but the killer, running across a second roof. He was getting away. Maya knew what she had to do, but it still took her a second to steel herself to do it.

Then she ran for the edge of the roof, building up as much speed as she could. Maya felt her foot slam down on the very edge and she pushed off as hard as she could, leaping out into space after the killer.

As she hung there in the space between the buildings, Maya had plenty of time to feel the terror of what might happen if her leap fell short, if she suddenly plummeted to the ground.

The strange thing was that the fear for herself was the smallest part of it. There was fear for her sister, because if Maya didn't make this, didn't catch up to the fleeing figure of the killer, then Megan was dead.

She found herself thinking of Marco as well. The thought of losing him like this, to an ill-timed jump… it was almost too much to bear.

Then Maya hit the roof on the far side of her leap, rolling to absorb some of the impact. She came up and kept running. The killer was ahead of her now, making his way across a couple of boards that had been bolted in place between two more of the roofs, obviously providing a way for employees working at one to access the other.

There were more ventilation ducts here, as well as several brick structures that appeared to be there to provide additional workspaces. Maya saw the killer duck out of sight behind one of them. He was only out of sight for an instant or two, but it was still enough to make Maya speed up, determined not to give him a chance to escape. She took the corner of the building fast, her Glock held close to her.

The killer had vanished.

Maya looked around quickly, taking out a flashlight so that she could get a better view than the moonlight provided. Unlike when she'd been searching for Neil Cooper, it didn't matter here if she gave away her position. There was no time for a prolonged search. It was less than five minutes to midnight now, which meant that Maya only had that time in which to take down the killer. She had to find him *now*.

Maya started to scan the rooftop carefully, checking each vent, each brick building, determined to be systematic even with the short time that she had in which to find her quarry. She flicked the beam of the flashlight from one hiding spot to the next, swiftly eliminating each one. She moved around a vent, checking for any sign of the killer.

The only good part was that there didn't seem to be any way off the roof other than the way Maya had come onto it. So long as Maya kept one eye on the makeshift bridge between the two buildings, she had the killer trapped.

"You might as well come out," she said. Maya doubted that it would work, but she figured it was worth a shot. "You don't have anywhere to go."

Was she really expecting the killer to come out from his hiding place with hands up? It was possible if he realized that it was his best shot to come out of this safely, but would a man who had cold-bloodedly killed three people and who had been about to kill a fourth give up that easily?

"This doesn't have to end badly," Maya said. "I have a gun, you have a knife. You can't fight your way out. It's better to give up peacefully."

Her flashlight continued the work of flicking from spot to spot, taking away each hiding place in turn. At last, there was only one left, in the form of one of those brick-built sheds set on top of the roof.

Maya started to move over to it, keeping it covered with her weapon and her flashlight, training the two on the same spot as she advanced. The killer had to be there. There was nowhere else.

Maya moved up to it, keeping her distance as she moved around it so that there would be no chance of a sudden spring from the killer getting close to her with the knife. She needed to end this cleanly. She didn't have enough time for anything more complicated.

"Freeze!" Maya said, leaping around the corner to cover the spot where she knew the killer had to be standing.

Only, she realized with a sudden sinking feeling, he wasn't there. The spot where he should have been was empty. Maya had been wrong, but she *couldn't* be wrong, because there was nowhere else he could be when Maya had checked every other hiding spot on the roof.

Maya listened intently. Somewhere a little way off, she could hear the sound of a car against the stillness of the night, but it was any sounds closer to her that she was interested in. Had the killer tried to make a run for it?

Maya tried to think. The killer must have been here, but she hadn't exactly been subtle about approaching the shed. If he'd timed it right, the killer could have slipped around the structure even as Maya did, keeping it between him and her. Which meant…

Maya was already turning as she heard the scrape of a shoe right behind her. She saw the flash of a knife against the night sky and tried to raise her gun, but the killer's weapon was already on its way down. Maya had to lift her flashlight to block the knife slash, and in that moment, the killer smashed into her, sending the gun clattering away across the roof into the darkness.

Maya had no time to try to grab for it, because it was all she could do to keep the killer from stabbing her in those first few moments. The two of them were pressed at close quarters, Maya's flashlight jammed against the blade of the knife while the killer struck at her with his free hand. Maya struck back with a knee, then reached up, wrenching away the mask that he wore.

A pale, thin face stood revealed in the moonlight, hatred etched on it.

"You bitch! You took away my chance to sacrifice her at the right time! But it doesn't matter. I'll kill you, then go back for her! It will be close enough. It has to be!"

"You're too late," Maya said, even though she knew she was the one running out of time. "You might as well give this up."

She punctuated her words with a blow from her elbow that bought her a moment to try to think, but the killer was on her immediately, striking with the knife again. Maya was grateful for the size of her flashlight, because it meant that she could use it like a club, blocking the blow and trying to strike back.

Then it occurred to her that she had a better option. She turned the flashlight, shining it straight into the killer's eyes. He staggered back, momentarily blinded, and Maya circled him, trying to work out the best way to take him down.

"I'll kill you," he promised, holding the knife out in front of himself. He didn't lunge forward at Maya though, and she knew that was a problem. If he overcommitted, Maya might have a chance to slam the flashlight down on his arm and disarm him, but as it was, he was waiting for her.

She didn't have any time to hold back, not with midnight approaching so quickly. She had to act, had to take the killer down, had to find a way to end this. Hoping against hope that it was a good idea, Maya threw herself forward at her opponent.

He lifted the knife, but Maya managed to slam the flashlight into the hand holding it, forcing him to drop it. She was in close with the killer then, his hands and hers somehow locked on the flashlight together like it was a weapon that they were fighting for control of. Maya tried to lash out with her head and knees, tried to fight in close with everything she had, but it was hard when she was already in pain from the lingering effects of the Moonlight Killer's bullet.

That was when the killer in front of Maya let go of the flashlight with one hand, slamming his fist into her side. He couldn't have known that was where Maya was injured, but his fist connected with the same spot the bullet had struck nonetheless, the sheer agony of it making Maya double over.

The killer was on her then, bearing her to the ground right at the edge of the building. He had the flashlight now, driving it against Maya's throat in an attempt to choke her, or force her over the edge, or both. She didn't have the strength then to fight back. She couldn't do it. The pain was too much.

"Die!" he snarled.

Then there was another figure there above Maya, lit perfectly by the moonlight. Maya had a moment to see Marco and then he was dragging the killer off her, throwing him down on the rooftop. The two of them wrestled, each trying to best the other, blows punctuating every shift of position.

Maya could see the killer reaching for the knife. It lay only just out of his reach, his fingers questing for it as Marco tried to hold him down. If he got to it…

Maya gritted her teeth, ignoring the pain as she got to her feet. She stepped forward and kicked the knife away, into the center of the roof. She made a grab for the killer's arm, holding onto it with all her strength while Marco grabbed his other arm. Between them, they managed to wrench his arms behind his back so that Marco could cuff him.

"You're under arrest," Maya said, but even then, it wasn't done. She checked her watch. There was just one more minute to midnight. Maya got out her phone, calling the Chesterford PD's main switchboard, hoping against hope that the Moonlight Killer would be listening in to that now that he didn't have a bug on her phone.

"Chesterford PD, how can I help you?"

"This is Agent Maya Grey with the FBI. I've just caught the killer. I repeat, I have the killer in custody, caught red-handed."

She could only hope that it would be enough to save her sister.

CHAPTER TWENTY FIVE

Maya sat in the hospital, wincing as once of the nurses there re-sewed her stitches. She'd popped several of them today between chasing after suspects and fighting on the rooftop.

Marco was there, watching her with the kind of concern that went beyond that of a partner or a friend.

"I was worried about you," he said. "When I heard you'd gone off alone…"

"I couldn't risk both of us on a theory that might not pan out," Maya replied. "What if, as soon as I left, Neil Cooper had been ready to confess?"

"So instead, you ran off alone to take on a killer, almost dying when you had to fight him on a rooftop?"

Maya put a hand on his. "But you found me in time. *How* did you find me?"

She'd texted him the general location, but that was different from finding her on one specific rooftop.

"When I got there, I saw the victim tied in place. Then I saw your flashlight beam up there. After that, it was just a question of trying to get to you in time."

He had, barely. Maya didn't want to think about what could have happened if he'd been only a few seconds later. Maybe Maya would have been able to find a way to fight her way out of it, but maybe she would have gone tumbling off the roof the way the killer intended. Maybe she would have been able to bring him down, but the time it took would have taken her past the deadline the Moonlight Killer had set.

"How is Aurora?" Maya asked the nurse. They'd brought the woman who would have been the killer's next victim back to the hospital, but hadn't been able to stay with her thanks to Maya's own injuries.

"The woman you brought in?" the nurse said. "She'll be fine. There's a sedative in her system and she has a few bruises, but she'll recover. We're keeping her hydrated, trying to flush the sedative from her system."

That was good. Maya had been focused on taking down the killer, but the well-being of his victim was what mattered. She and Marco had saved a woman's life, stopping her from being killed to turn her into a moondial, pointing to the time when the next victim would be killed.

"There," the nurse said as she finished her work. "You're all sewn up, Agent Grey. Try to take it easy this time. These things take time to heal."

Maya wished that she could promise that she was going to be able to take it easy from now on, but this wasn't done. They'd caught one killer, but the Moonlight Killer was still out there somewhere. He still had her sister in his hands.

She got up, heading out of the hospital room. Even as she did so, her phone rang. It was Agent Swift, her new boss, the head of the task force hunting for the Moonlight Killer.

It seemed strange, her boss calling her so late. It was well past midnight now, a time when Maya might have expected Agent Swift to be home in bed, but even as she answered the call, Maya could guess what she was calling about.

"Agent Swift?" Maya said.

"Grey, what's the situation over in Chesterford?"

"We managed to catch the killer," Maya said. "He's in custody now and his last victim is safe."

"All good things," Swift replied, "but what about the main case? Has there been any contact from the Moonlight Killer yet?"

"Not yet, but it's only been a couple of hours," Maya pointed out. "It may take him longer to deliver one of his postcards now that his main base of operations is destroyed."

"But you're expecting that contact?"

That was a worrying question. *Could* Maya expect the Moonlight Killer to get in touch with her? She'd solved the case before the deadline, but it had been so close. What if the Moonlight Killer thought that she'd gone past that deadline? If he did, then Megan might already be dead.

No, Maya couldn't think like that. She had to believe that this might still work out well.

"I met his deadline, and he's kept his word so far. I expect him to get in touch with a release site for my sister."

"And you think that's all that will happen?" Agent Swift asked. "Your sister is his last hostage, and he's going to be angry that you destroyed his operation. My guess is that he'll want to try to get revenge on you."

"You don't sound worried about that, ma'am," Maya said.

"I think it also gives us our best chance of taking him down. I imagine you've thought the same, Grey."

Maya had. She didn't want the Moonlight Killer to simply vanish. She wanted to stop him, to arrest him, but she wanted her sister back safely even more. Did she really believe the same of Agent Swift?

"I've thought about it," Maya said. "Although we've built up some evidence about his identity through this case."

"Not enough to work out who he is," Agent Swift replied. "We know he's ex–Special Forces, we know that he's smart, we know where his bunker was, and maybe we'll find out more from that. But it's not enough. Our best chance to take him down is now, at the end of all of this."

"And my sister?" Maya asked.

"I'm not Harris," Swift said. "We'll take every precaution to make sure that your sister is okay. But we have to take down the Moonlight Killer, or more people will die. When he gets in touch, you'll contact me immediately."

It was an instruction, not a question.

"Yes, ma'am," Maya said.

"Okay," Swift said. "Take the time before he gets in touch to rest and prepare. I'll see you back at the department in a couple of days."

She hung up.

Marco looked over at Maya. "Swift?"

Maya nodded. "Just checking to see if there was any news from the Moonlight Killer yet."

Marco came up to her and held her close for a moment. "He'll get in touch. You were in time, Maya."

Maya hoped so. The alternative… it was too much to think about.

She sighed. "Come on. Let's go home."

*

Maya sat in her apartment, worrying and waiting. It had been two days now since she'd caught the killer. Two days since she and Marco had saved his victim, Aurora. Two days since Maya had called frantically over the open channel of the Chesterford PD that she and Marco had caught the killer, hoping that the Moonlight Killer would be listening in.

"He should have gotten in touch by now," Maya said.

Across her apartment, Marco was making them both coffee. He'd stayed with her since they both got back, almost like he didn't dare leave her alone in her apartment, or maybe just because he wanted to be with her. Maya was more than happy to have him there in her apartment, in her life, and not just because of how much had grown between the two of them. His presence there was keeping her from going insane with worry, but only just.

"He's waited before sending us a location before," Marco reassured her.

"But what if this isn't that?" Maya demanded. "What if he's decided that he's gotten everything he wants, so he can just kill Megan?"

"He's kept his word so far," Marco pointed out. "You've always been prepared to trust in that, even when everyone else has been worried that he'll betray us by killing his victims."

This wasn't the same, though. Before, the Moonlight Killer had needed Maya to continue doing what he wanted. If he'd killed his hostages rather than letting them go according to the rules of his game, he'd known that Maya wouldn't keep investigating cases for him.

"I've investigated the last case for him," Maya said. "He knows he can't force me to do more, because then I won't trust that he'll ever release Megan."

"He might kidnap more women," Marco pointed out. "He kidnapped twelve for a reason. Maybe he'll try to force you to finish the sequence."

"But if he doesn't do that, then he has no reason to keep Megan alive."

"Except for the rules of his game," Marco replied.

That was enough to make Maya pause, because he had a point. The Moonlight Killer seemed to be obsessed with his game and with his rules. Those rules demanded that he should let Megan go. That was enough to give Maya a little hope, but it was only a little. It made her willing to sit there, waiting, especially if that waiting was alongside Marco.

Even so, it was hard to ignore the worry that any message from the Moonlight Killer might just be to tell her where to find her sister's body.

Even as Maya thought that, a knock came on the door to her apartment. Maya rushed over to the door, throwing it open. There on the floor outside the apartment was a postcard.

The Moonlight Killer had sent her a message.

Maya snatched up the postcard hungrily, holding it up to the light to look at it. On the front, the Moonlight Killer had drawn another of his infuriating pictures. A bunny rabbit was tied to a tree, looking out pleadingly from the card.

On the reverse, there were GPS coordinates written out, along with a brief message.

Dear Maya,

You succeeded just in time. Well done. You've earned your reward. It's time to bring this to an end. If you want your sister back, come to the coordinates on this card at 9pm today. Come alone. Not Detective Spinelli, not FBI backup. Alone, or she dies. I will know.

The Moonlight Killer

That sign-off was enough to make Maya pause. He'd never done it before. Was it just an acknowledgment that everyone knew by now who was behind the kidnappings? Was it an attempt to make Maya afraid? If so, it was working.

Maya passed the card to Marco, who read it.

"There's no way that you're doing this alone," he said.

Maya looked him in the eye. "You know that I have to. You know that there isn't a choice."

"I could follow discreetly," Marco suggested.

"When he's shown how good he is at surveillance before? He's ex-military. He'll spot you."

"Then we do it electronically," Marco insisted. "We contact Swift. We send you in wearing a camera. We have backup nearby. When you have your sister, we move in."

Again, Maya had to shake her head. She took both of Marco's hands.

"Marco, you know that I can't. I know you're trying to protect me, but you can't, not from this. I have to go in alone. I have to get my sister back."

"And if this is all a trap?" Marco asked.

Maya was almost certain that it would be, but she had to do this anyway.

"Then the Moonlight Killer had better make sure that it works. Tonight's the night when I'm going to take him down."

CHAPTER TWENTY SIX

Maya was as prepared as she could be as she entered the stretch of woodland the Moonlight Killer's coordinates led to. Even so, she could feel her fear rising like the full moon rising overhead. She was going up against a deadly serial killer, and she had no choice but to do this alone.

Maya was wearing a tactical vest and she had a long rifle with her as well as her Glock. Marco was waiting back on the edges of the woodland too, ready to come rushing to back Maya up if she called him. He would also be the one to call Swift to let her know what was happening if this went wrong. None of it did anything to dissipate the tension that Maya could feel running through her as she moved forward.

The forest around her was dark, only Maya's flashlight and the silvery moon overhead providing any illumination. Maya had driven as close as she could to the spot the postcard indicated, but now she had to approach on foot, along a trail barely wide enough for a single person. Maya moved slowly, checking the ground in front of her for traps.

A part of her was sure that this whole thing was a trap. The Moonlight Killer had sent her a location, and it was possible that he would keep his word by releasing her sister, but Maya didn't believe for a moment that doing so would be the end of this. The two of them had been locked in a battle of wits and wills for so long now that Maya didn't see this ending any other way than with a confrontation between the two of them.

In that confrontation, Maya knew that she wouldn't be able to hold back. The last time she and the Moonlight Killer had come face to face, they had been fighting with lethal intent. Maya knew that she couldn't hesitate. If she could bring the Moonlight Killer in alive, that would be amazing, but if he fought back, she would have to use lethal force just to survive.

That was another reason she'd left Marco on the edge of the forest. Maya didn't want him to see her like this, ready to kill if that was what it took. Some people had to be stopped. The moment the Moonlight Killer had taken her sister, Maya and he had been heading toward one another inexorably, set on a collision course.

For now, though, Maya had to focus on getting to the spot the postcard indicated. It was almost nine p.m., and Maya didn't dare to be late, not when the Moonlight Killer had left several of the victims he'd released in spots where they would have died if Maya hadn't found them.

Was that what he would do here? Leave Megan in danger and let Maya try to find her in time? That would be within the rules of his sick game. So would trying to kill Maya while she attempted to free her sister from his clutches.

Ahead, Maya thought she could see a clearing. To her surprise, it was lit, illuminated by the light of a campfire. Was Maya about to stumble into someone's campsite? Had she gone to the wrong place? Or was this a piece of set dressing by the Moonlight Killer, trying to make everything look cozy and calm when in fact he was getting ready to strike at Maya?

Then Maya saw the figure tied to a tree, there on the edge of the clearing, and her heart beat faster.

"Megan!" Maya called out, unable to help herself, even though all her training said that she should keep quiet, approach with caution.

She saw the woman's head rise in recognition, although her back was to Maya so she couldn't look Maya's way. Maya moved in as quickly as she dared, wanting to get to her sister, wanting to free her from the ropes which wrapped around the tree, obviously holding Megan in place so that she couldn't run.

Maya checked for tripwires and pressure plates as she moved forward. The Moonlight Killer had used explosive traps in the past. Maya wouldn't put it past him to tie her sister there as bait, letting Maya trigger an explosion that would kill both her and her sister if she moved too quickly.

There didn't seem to be any wires, though, or anything that might harm her as she approached the clearing. Was it possible that the Moonlight Killer was going to keep his word? Was his plan simply to hand over Megan and disappear, knowing that there wasn't enough evidence to track him or identify him?

Maya didn't believe that, but she didn't know what else to think as she approached the tree.

Megan was standing there in a gray jumpsuit, the same as when Maya had last seen her, her head down again, her hands behind her back where they'd been tied.

"Hold on, Megan," Maya said. "I'll have you free in a second or two."

Maya set down her rifle against the tree. She went around to Megan's hands, ready to untie her. That was when she realized that her hands *weren't* tied. And one of those hands held a syringe. She lashed out with it, and Maya barely dodged in time.

"Megan?" Only it *wasn't* Megan. It was a completely different woman, with a similar build, similar hair, but there was nothing close about their features. This woman's features were currently a mask of hatred and determination there to do Maya harm.

She lunged at Maya again with the syringe. What was in it? Poison? A sedative? Maya didn't want to find out, certainly not by letting her simply inject Maya with it. Maya twisted out of the way, avoiding the attack again.

The woman struck out at her with fists and feet then, throwing a kick at Maya's midsection, then swinging a punch toward her head. Maya blocked the first and ducked the second, striking back with a punch to the woman's jaw that made her stagger.

The woman thrust out with the syringe again, stopping Maya from following up as quickly as she wanted to. It wasn't quite as dangerous as fighting against someone with a knife, but it was still a weapon Maya couldn't allow to get close to her.

The woman lunged at her again. Maya blocked the thrust of the syringe, then kicked the woman in the knee, making her stumble. She wrenched at the woman's arm, forcing her to drop the syringe. Maya stamped on it, shattering it and spilling the contents over the forest floor.

The woman saw that and looked briefly scared, then determined. Maya saw her look over to the rifle Maya had left by the tree. She lunged for it, obviously determined to get to it to use it against Maya.

Maya got to it at the same time that the other woman did, the two of them getting their hands on the weapon in the same moment. They wrestled over it, but Maya could feel that she was the one with the greater strength.

"What was the plan?" Maya demanded, as she kept fighting. "Did he send you to kill me?"

"I'm just here to deliver you. You pissed someone off, and he wants you bad."

"So, you're… what? A bounty hunter or something?"

"Something like that." The woman feinted a headbutt, then lashed out with a kick that caught Maya on the thigh.

A hired gun. Exactly the kind of person the Moonlight Killer preferred to use. Someone he could pay anonymously.

Maya struck back with a knee, then wrenched the gun sideways, breaking the other woman's grip. She brought the weapon around, slamming the butt of it into the woman's skull and knocking her to the ground, where she knelt for a second or two, as though stunned. Maya wasn't fooled by it. She brought the rifle up to her shoulder, leveling it at her attacker.

"Don't move," Maya warned her.

The woman stood. "I'm unarmed."

"Do you think I'm going to believe that?" Maya said. "If you're really a bounty hunter, you'll have *something*."

The woman started to take a step forward. Maya fired then, a warning shot aimed at the ground between her feet. "Hands up. Do you think for one moment I won't shoot?"

The woman seemed to consider that for a moment or two, and must have seen the determination on Maya's face, because she raised her hands, taking a step back.

"Did he tell you that I'm FBI?" Maya asked. "Do you know what *he* is? Do you know that you're being paid to deliver an FBI agent to a serial killer?"

"I take people where I'm paid to take them," the woman said.

"In this case, doing it will see you in jail, unless you give me answers. Do you *like* working for the Moonlight Killer?"

That got a reaction where Maya's other words hadn't been able to. Maya saw her blanch slightly at the sound of the Moonlight Killer's nickname. She obviously hadn't known who she was working for.

"Oh, you didn't know that?" Maya said. "You didn't know that you're working for a man who has murdered woman after woman, strangling them under the full moon? Do you know what happened to the last person he hired? There was a PI he was using to follow me and my partner. She ended up dead. How do you want this night to end?"

"What do you want?" the bounty hunter asked. "You're talking to me like you're trying to convince me, rather than just taking me in."

"Where is he?" Maya asked.

She shook her head. "You know that I don't know that. If you've been hunting this guy, you know that he's a ghost."

Maya knew that. She'd learned exactly how hard finding the Moonlight Killer could be, exactly how easily he melted away, leaving no trace of himself behind. She'd seen him use cutouts before, people who didn't know who they were working for, who were paid anonymously. The bounty hunter was just one more of those.

Yet there was still one way that she might prove useful.

"Where were you supposed to take me?" Maya demanded. "He wanted you to kidnap me and bring me to him, right? So *where* were you supposed to take me?"

"To the farm," the bounty hunter said.

"*What* farm?" Maya said. There were probably dozens of farms and small acreages in the area. She needed more information.

The bounty hunter opened her mouth to reply, and that was when Maya saw blood bloom on her chest. At the same moment, Maya heard the sound of a shot echoing through the forest. She saw the bounty hunter collapse, clearly dead even before she hit the ground. Maya flung herself into cover among the trees, because more shots came, tearing bark from the trees around Maya.

The Moonlight Killer, it had to be. Yes, he could have hired someone to do this part, but Maya didn't believe he would. He would want to do this part himself. He was ex-military, too, so he had the skills to pick off a target from a distance.

Another shot came. Maya tried to pinpoint the direction. She knew that she couldn't stay behind the tree she was using for cover all night. She had to get to him.

More than that, he was giving her a clue to his location. Keeping her head down, moving from cover to cover, Maya set off in the direction that the Moonlight Killer had been firing from.

CHAPTER TWENTY SEVEN

Maya moved forward carefully, rifle held ready to bring up and fire the moment she saw any threat. Through the canopy of trees, Maya saw the full moon hanging above, reflected light shining down on her.

Its presence added to her fear. The Moonlight Killer famously killed his victims under the full moon. He'd lured Maya here for this. He'd brought her to this place for some final confrontation, one where he thought that he would kill Maya.

Maya couldn't let that happen.

Was her sister alive? Did the Moonlight Killer need Megan anymore? Maya's fear was that he might already have strangled her, deciding that Maya would come after him regardless.

Maya felt her anger rising then, alongside her fear. After everything that the Moonlight Killer had done, a part of her wanted to kill him. In that moment, she felt herself slipping away from the mindset of an FBI agent, back into the attitude she'd had when she'd been in military intelligence.

Back then, it hadn't been about suspects and arrests, bringing people in alive whatever the cost. Then, there had been only objectives to achieve, targets who needed to be found and killed. In Maya's mind, the Moonlight Killer was starting to slip from being a suspect to arrest to being a target to destroy, her anger overwhelming almost everything.

Maya stalked on through the forest, moving carefully by the light of the moon, not daring to give away her position with her flashlight.

She found the first trap a little later: a snare laid on the ground, larger than one that might have been set for most animals. Maya moved around it carefully and stopped as the moonlight reflected off the silvery wire leading to a claymore mine.

The Moonlight Killer clearly wasn't holding back with her now.

Maya moved past the claymore mine, and that was when another shot came, splintering the bark of a tree near her head. Some of those splinters dug into her flesh, drawing blood in a sudden, sharp pain. Maya ignored it, kept her head low, and fired back in the direction the shot had come from. She moved into cover, then crawled, popping up with her rifle, trying to spot any sign of her suspect through the night sight fitted to the top.

Instinct made Maya duck down again sharply and another shot came, tearing up a tree trunk behind Maya. The Moonlight Killer had only missed her by inches this time.

Maya moved forward, slipping through the night in silence, heading in the direction the shots had come from. She found another claymore mine laid across her path and carefully disarmed it, not wanting to leave it where it might catch her or Megan on the way out of this.

Because they *were* going to get out of this. Maya was determined about that. If her sister was alive, then Maya was going to get to her and get her out of there.

To do that, though, Maya needed to *find* her sister. The best way to do that was to follow the Moonlight Killer through the forest, hunting him even as he hunted her.

The stress of the deadly cat-and-mouse game made Maya look around nervously. Every twitch of a branch or rustle of a leaf became a sign that the Moonlight Killer was there, making Maya swing around, leveling her weapon to meet the threat. Maya had to tell herself to stop reacting, knowing that the Moonlight Killer would be able to take advantage of it if Maya kept jumping at every shadow.

Was he still hunting her with whatever sniper rifle he was using? Or was he stalking through the dark now with a length of rope in his hands, determined to strangle Maya the way he strangled his other victims?

Did he view her as a victim to kill that way, or was she an opponent to be taken down in whatever way he could? He'd been quick enough to fire back at her in the bunker.

Maya couldn't take the risk of assuming that she was safe, especially when several of the Moonlight Killer's shots had come so close to hitting her. She had to move from cover to cover, trying to make sure that she didn't give anyone watching a chance to get a clean shot at her.

It meant that she couldn't move at full speed through the forest, especially not when the Moonlight Killer had already shown that he was prepared to leave traps behind to try to kill Maya if she was unwary. She had to plan every sequence of steps she took across the forest until, somewhere ahead of her, she saw another clearing, with another campfire.

Maya closed in carefully, knowing that it was likely to be a trap. She moved around the edge of the clearing, making sure that there were no explosives set there. It also allowed her to look into it without being seen.

There was a sniper rifle there, resting against a lawn chair, a postcard stuck to the barrel. Maya moved forward cautiously, knowing that this could be a trap, a way to lure her into position so that the Moonlight Killer would have a clear shot at her.

Maya snatched it up and then threw herself into cover, half-expecting the Moonlight Killer to start shooting at her even as she snatched it. She rolled as she hit the forest floor, hearing twigs break as she landed. Maya came up, ready to fight, expecting that the Moonlight Killer would be coming at her if he wasn't shooting.

Instead, there was only stillness and silence in the forest, leaving Maya feeling a little embarrassed that she'd reacted so strongly. She took the postcard, reading it by the light coming from the campfire. There was a picture on the front of a bunny rabbit sitting atop a cartoon bomb, a larger rabbit off to one side holding a length of strangling rope and wearing a mask. On the back were just four words:

Find us by midnight.

Maya cursed the fact that even now, the Moonlight Killer was keeping up his games. He was still treating this like it was some whimsical competition between them, rather than a life or death struggle in which Megan's life hung in the balance.

Then she realized what this postcard meant, what the sniper rifle in the clearing meant: it meant that the Moonlight Killer wasn't hunting her through the forest anymore. He was waiting for her instead, with Megan.

Which meant that Maya couldn't just follow him back to her sister.

That was a worrying thought. Maya started to look around the clearing, looking for tracks, looking for anything that would let her spot the direction the Moonlight Killer had gone in. A part of her expected him to deliberately leave a trail for Maya to follow.

There was nothing. Any tracks he'd made, he'd been careful to disguise or confuse, so that there was nothing to follow, no way of letting him lead her back to his location.

Did that mean that Maya was meant to blunder around this forest blindly, hoping that she came across the Moonlight Killer's lair before his deadline ran out? Was she supposed to hunt randomly for him and Megan, following whatever seemed like the most likely route?

Then Maya realized that she didn't have to. What had the bounty hunter said before the Moonlight Killer shot her? That she'd been paid to take Maya back to "the farm"?

Maya got out her phone, hoping there would be enough reception for her to do this. There was, just. She started to look for any farms in the vicinity of the spot where she stood. The problem wasn't finding a farm, but the fact that there seemed to be so many of them.

There were at least ten or so in the surrounding area, some further than others, but none of them a problem if the Moonlight Killer had a vehicle with him. Which meant that Maya had to work out which one was the one the bounty hunter had meant.

Maya started to look at the farms, trying to see if there was anything to differentiate one from another. Yet how was she meant to tell the difference between Hazel Tree Farm, Dovecote Farm, Twelve Warrens Farm…

Wait, Twelve Warrens Farm?

Maya had learned plenty of things about the Moonlight Killer in the period while she'd been solving cases at his behest. One of those things was his obsession with twelves. Twelve women, twelve cases, now twelve warrens, when he'd called his hostages bunnies? Had he *really* done something like that, been so obvious about it?

Yet it was only obvious because Maya had been looking. She quickly used her phone to do some research, and found that Twelve Warrens Farm had been bought through an anonymous holdings group a few years ago and renamed from Hanratty's Farm. It had been empty before that, sold after the sudden, accidental death of the former owners. One of the newspaper articles from the time mentioned their son, Michael Francis Hanratty, who had been away in the army at the time of the deaths.

Had he? Or had Maya just found out about the Moonlight Killer's first victims? Had she just found out more about him than she had ever thought she might know?

The enormity of that made her breath catch in her throat. The Moonlight Killer had come out and given her his identity, just like that. He must have known what Maya would be able to do with the information. It was his way of luring her closer, drawing her in, giving her a shot to bring him down.

And it was obvious that he didn't expect Maya to survive the attempt. Why else give away his identity like that? He clearly thought that he was going to be able to kill Maya, to kill anyone who came for him.

Or maybe he was planning to disappear. Maybe he would change his name after this, start again under another identity somewhere else. It was obvious that he had the skills to do it. Once he did so, even knowing the truth of his identity wouldn't help very much.

Maya stood there for several seconds, then made a phone call.

Marco picked up after only a single ring, obviously waiting for her.

"Maya?"

"Michael Francis Hanratty. That's his name, Marco. If I don't make it out of this, that's his name."

"Maya, wait, you're worrying me."

"And Marco? I love you." They were words she should have said before. She should have at least confessed her feelings in some other form. Now, it seemed almost too late.

Maya hung up before Marco could say anything else. It was time for her to go to Twelve Warrens Farm and finish this, once and for all.

CHAPTER TWENTY EIGHT

Maya could see the farm ahead now, lights visible within the farmhouse. The whole place seemed dilapidated to the point where, if there hadn't been those lights, she might not have believed that it was occupied, outbuildings seeming as though they might fall down at any moment.

Maya wondered how much of that was a deliberate ploy to keep people away and how much was simply that the Moonlight Killer hadn't been back there in years.

Maya had a name for him now. Michael Francis Hanratty. That was the man who had terrorized so many people over the years. That was the man who had killed so many women on the full moon, taken away their lives at the moment when they were about to transition to become something more.

Maya could only feel hatred for a man like that, especially when he had her sister in his clutches. That hatred, that burning anger, made a part of her want to charge forward into the farm, gun ready to take the Moonlight Killer down the moment she saw him.

Maya moved forward more cautiously instead, padding toward the farm on silent feet with her rifle raised, ready for trouble. She kept a careful eye on the ground as she advanced, ready for any traps that the Moonlight Killer might have left in her path.

The Moonlight Killer. Even now that she knew his real name, Maya couldn't help thinking of him that way. He had been this nameless boogeyman for so long that it almost seemed wrong to give him a name. Maya certainly wouldn't dignify him with one as she approached this conflict. A name meant that she had to spend time thinking about everything that might have brought him to that point. Maya wanted to focus on what would happen in the minutes to follow.

She didn't find any tripwires, pressure plates, or sensors as she moved into the farm. The Moonlight Killer seemed to have left the path open for her to approach, which only made Maya more nervous.

Did he think she wouldn't find him? No, that didn't make any sense, not when he'd given the farm such an obvious name to lure her in. The only explanation that seemed to work was that the Moonlight Killer wanted her to come to him. He wanted this confrontation as much as Maya did. He wanted it here. The whole farm was the trap and Maya was walking into it.

She had no choice, not with her sister's life on the line.

Maya moved forward, toward the house. She wasn't about to take chances, but she knew that the farmhouse was where this was going to end. The Moonlight Killer had left lights on there for a reason. That was where he wanted the end of all of this to happen.

The full moon continued to shine down on Maya, reminding her that the Moonlight Killer had probably planned all of this from the start. He'd been building up to some version of this moment from the instant that he first kidnapped Megan, maybe even before that. Perhaps the two of them had always been on some kind of collision course with one another.

Now, as Maya stalked up to the farmhouse, a figure stepped out of it. He was tall and broad shouldered, with dark hair and dressed in dark combat fatigues that he'd obviously used to blend into the forest. He was holding a length of rope in one hand, but had no other obvious weapons.

That was the only thing that kept Maya from shooting him as soon as she saw him. If he'd had a gun in his hand, Maya wouldn't have hesitated, wouldn't have *dared* to hesitate with such a dangerous man. As it was, though, she paused in the shadow of one of the outbuildings.

That gave her the time to realize something: he wasn't wearing a mask. Lit as he was by the lights of the house, Maya could see his handsome, square-jawed features with the most piercing blue eyes she had ever seen.

"You might as well come out, Maya," the Moonlight Killer said. "I know you're there."

Maya stepped out with her rifle raised, covering him. The moment he moved, the moment he gave her any kind of excuse, she would open fire. It wasn't just the threat that the serial killer represented, it was everything he'd done to her over the last few weeks, everything he'd done to so many people.

"Stay where you are," Maya told him. "If you move even an inch, I'll kill you."

"That would be unwise, Maya," he said. He raised his hands like he was surrendering. "Look at my left wrist."

There was something there, something that blinked with a steady light. Maya knew what she was looking at immediately.

"Another dead man's switch?"

The Moonlight Killer nodded in response to that. "This one linked to my vital signs. If you kill me, then an explosive device triggers. One that is currently attached to the seat to which your sister is tied. Oh, and there's a manual trigger. If you don't put your guns away, I'll set it off anyway."

Maya swallowed, feeling a fresh rush of fear running through her. She had thought that this moment would be simple, yet the Moonlight Killer had sprung another surprise on her. She tried to think of something that would buy her time, let her work out what her options were. She set aside the rifle, knowing that it would be useless to her when she didn't dare to kill the man who stood before her. She didn't dare risk trying for a non-lethal shot, when there was too much of a chance of that going wrong.

"Is this where you killed your first people?" Maya asked.

"My parents?" The Moonlight Killer shrugged as he said it. "You need to come up with something more interesting than that if you want to keep my attention, Maya. I *gave* you that information with the name of the farm."

He made it sound like it had been obvious and simple, rather than a puzzle that Maya had solved. He'd known that she would make the connection to the name of the farm, and he'd known that Maya would then do the additional research to find out about him. He'd been a step ahead of her at every stage, just as he had been through so much of this investigation.

"Then why give me that information, Michael?" Maya asked. "Why did you want me to know it all?"

He smiled then. "I go by Frank these days. But well done for asking a more interesting question. Why did I want you to know? Because I find you fascinating, Maya. Because you have a fine brain, one very nearly as good as my own. Perhaps I want you to know me better, before you die."

He slid that part in as casually as if they were talking about what a fine night it was.

"That's where this has been heading from the start, hasn't it?" Maya said.

"Ah, a dull question, given that you already know the answer, but I'll indulge you. Yes. You have changed considerably, after all, and I like to take my victims right at that point, right at the moment when the moon is due to change."

"Why is that?" Maya asked. "What is it about them changing that offends you so much?"

He narrowed his eyes then. "Offends me? Have you understood so little? They're perfect in that moment. They have so much potential. And then they spoil it. They go on to try great things, and they fail. Take them now, on the cusp of change, and they're forever in that state when they *could* be anything. Take you. What will you do if you come through this? You *could* become something great, but you won't, will you? You'll mess up your relationship with the detective. You'll get yourself fired from your job. You're brilliant, Maya, but you'll find a way."

"Which is why you can't let me live?" Maya asked.

"You can live. You just have to kill me, and your sister, to stop me."

He charged at her then, with no warning, no hesitation. The suddenness of the change was like a snake striking after seeming totally relaxed. He slammed into Maya, the speed of the movement stunning. Maya was ready for his attack, though, and she twisted, throwing him over her hip so that he landed in the dirt of the farmyard.

The Moonlight Killer sprang back to his feet, coming at Maya again. He whipped the rope he held at her face, then threw a punch with his right hand that Maya barely blocked with her elbow. Even then, the force of it was painful, making her wince.

She lashed out with a foot, catching the Moonlight Killer on the side of the knee. That knee buckled for a moment and Maya heard her opponent make a small sound of pain. She moved in, throwing a couple of punches that grazed him, forcing him to keep moving back.

Maya kept pressing forward, not wanting to give up the initiative, but she realized too late that the Moonlight Killer was just luring her forward. He changed level and tackled her, blasting Maya from her feet with his momentum.

He landed on top of Maya, lashing out with his fists, forcing her to react. She turned in to him, trying to come up on a takedown of her own, trying to put him on the bottom. Somehow, the Moonlight Killer went with the movement, and now he was behind Maya, the rope he held whipping around her throat. Maya managed to get the fingers of her left hand in the way, but the Moonlight Killer still hauled back on the rope, his strength terrific, the rope starting to strangle Maya even though she tried to block the movement.

She couldn't breathe. There was a horrific pressure on her throat, enough that it made spots dance in front of Maya's eyes, darkness closing in on the edge of her vision.

"I thought you would be more of a challenge," the Moonlight Killer whispered to her. "Look at the moon as you die, Maya. See how beautiful it is as you die."

He wrenched Maya's neck back, forcing her to look up even as he strangled her. Maya found herself thinking about Marco in that moment, and about Megan. The thought of losing them made pain rise up in Maya, and grief…

…and anger.

Maya grabbed for her Glock, still in its holster. She cleared it.

"What are you going to do, Maya? If you kill me, you kill your sister."

Maya wasn't planning to kill him, though. She aimed downward by feel, setting the barrel against the Moonlight Killer's leg. Then she pulled the trigger.

He screamed as the shot sounded, both sounds loud against the silence of the night. Maya took the opportunity to wrench clear of the rope around her neck, even as the Moonlight Killer tried to hold on.

She kicked out at his leg then, right where she'd shot him, and that made the serial killer collapse to the ground. Maya was on him then, hitting him with her fists, with her elbows, even with the butt of her gun until he slumped in unconsciousness.

Maya grabbed for his wrist, looking at the device there. It seemed to be an adapted smartwatch of some kind, rigged up to send a message to the explosive device in the farmhouse.

Maya worked quickly finding the buttons that would turn it off. Only when she was sure that it was dark and silent did she rip it from the Moonlight Killer's wrist, tossing it away into the darkness.

Maya stepped away then, and she heard a groan as the Moonlight Killer started to regain consciousness. Maya took her Glock, leveling it at him, aiming right between his eyes.

"Are you going to shoot me, Maya?" he asked. "Remember your sister."

"Look at your wrist, Frank," she said.

She saw him look there, and for the first time, she saw a hint of fear on his face as he realized that Maya could shoot him without anything happening to her sister.

Would she? Maya's instincts said that she should. This was a man who had killed countless women, who had kidnapped Maya's sister, who had systematically beaten her, who had tried to kill Maya. Maya could feel her anger at that building, hardening into something cold and deadly, something that made her finger start to tighten on the trigger.

Then she thought about Marco, and what he would say if he were here. He wouldn't want Maya to do this. He would remind her that she was an FBI agent, that she had a duty.

Maya thought about Megan, too. Maya couldn't imagine her sister wanting to see Maya kill someone, even the man who had tormented her so much. Maya didn't want to be that person in front of her sister. She didn't want to be a killer like the one who had imprisoned her.

Maya took her finger off the trigger.

"Can't do it?" the Moonlight Killer asked with a sneer.

Maya stepped forward and kicked him in the face, sending him sprawling back into the dirt. She got out her handcuffs, snapping them around his wrists, attaching the cuffs to a beam on the farmhouse porch.

She got up and headed into the farmhouse. Maya felt relief flooding through her at the sight of Megan sitting there in the middle of the kitchen, tied to a chair. The emotion was almost overwhelming in that moment.

How long had it been since she had seen her sister in real life? More than a year, since she'd supposedly left for the trip that she never came back from. Maya rushed over to her, crouching beside her, working quickly to cut away the bonds that held her.

"Maya!" Megan threw her arms around Maya as soon as she was able to. "I knew you'd come."

Maya hugged her sister back tightly. "I'm just glad you're safe."

Maya took out her phone, making a call. It only took a couple of rings before a voice on the other end answered.

"Agent Grey?" Agent Swift said.

"Agent Swift? I need backup to my location. I've recovered the Moonlight Killer's last hostage, and he's under arrest."

"Say that again, Agent Grey?" Agent Swift said with a slight note of disbelief.

Maya took a breath.

"The Moonlight Killer is under arrest."

CHAPTER TWENTY NINE

Maya sat on a lawn chair in the garden, with Megan on another just across the table from her. Megan was in a light summer dress. Maya was wearing slacks and a cream shirt. Marco brought over drinks for the three of them: beer for him and Maya, white wine for Megan. The lawn spread out expansively around them.

"Your new place is amazing," Megan said, with a look back at the large suburban house that was Maya and Marco's new home.

"It will be once we finish unpacking," Maya said.

"Are you sure you can afford all of this?" Megan asked.

Marco answered that one. "Since Maya got promoted and I joined the FBI as more than a consultant, we can manage."

Promoted made it all sound so simple, when the months since arresting the Moonlight Killer had been anything *but* simple. There had been investigations, questions over Maya's methods, all stemming from Harris. Ultimately, though, the fact that Maya had caught the Moonlight Killer counted for more than anything. Harris had found himself quietly sidelined, while Maya…

Maya had her own department now.

"So, you have the house, you have the jobs," Megan said. "Is there any chance we'll be seeing a ring on your finger soon?"

Maya smiled at that, looking over to where Marco was starting to look a little embarrassed about it all. "Maybe, eventually. For now, it's enough that we have each other."

"How are things with you, Megan?" Marco asked, obviously trying to deflect attention from their personal lives. Maya was grateful for that. She and Marco would take things at their own pace. After everything they'd been through together, Maya was glad to have the time to do that.

Megan smiled. "I sold a couple of my art pieces to a gallery, and the art college says I can go back."

"I'm glad," Maya said, reaching out a hand to cover Megan's. It meant that her sister had a chance to start rebuilding her life, but Maya knew that it would never be as easy as that. "What about the… other part of it?"

"I'm still seeing the therapist if that's what you're asking," Megan said. "I think… I think it's helping. I'm going to see some of the others next weekend."

The others. Maya hadn't expected her sister to keep in touch with the other women who had been kept in the bunker with her, yet perhaps she *should* have anticipated that. Being stuck in such a small space together, undergoing such trauma together, it was inevitable that it would create a bond, wasn't it? Maybe it would help them, being able to meet up with the only other people who truly understood what they'd all been through.

Maya found herself wondering what their lives would be like now. Those of them who had survived. Maya wouldn't forget that two of the captive women had died, and that the Moonlight Killer had murdered several other people during all of this.

Yet Maya's thoughts were mostly with those women the Moonlight Killer had kidnapped, right at key moments of change in their lives. Would those women simply be able to slot back into their lives? Would they be able to make the changes they'd been dreaming of, or would the Moonlight Killer's cruelty ruin things for them? Maya could only hope not.

Maya could see a brief flicker of pain cross Megan's face, obviously as she thought about everything the Moonlight Killer had done to her. Maya squeezed her sister's hand again, a little harder this time.

"You're safe now. He's locked away in the most secure mental institution we could find. He's never going to get out." Maya didn't know if she was saying that purely for her sister's benefit or at least partly for her own, reminding herself that the man who had made her run around at his beck and call wasn't in a position to torment her anymore.

"It's strange to think that without all of this, a bunch of killers would still be out there walking free," Marco said, sipping his beer.

It was a reminder that, whatever the horrors of it all, some good had come out of it. The Moonlight Killer might have treated Maya like a puppet, there to dance this way and that at his whim, but the result of his threats and his deadly games was that Maya had found out the truth about multiple murders, had caught many serial killers, had allowed many families to finally achieve closure about the deaths of their loved ones.

That had been a part of Maya's job that she'd always felt was important. The part that she'd found the most fulfilling. It was the reason why she'd spent so much of her time working on cold cases, why she'd put so much effort into trying to find answers about long-past crimes.

Maya was still thinking about that when her phone started to ring. Maya saw Samit's name on the display.

"Even today?" Megan asked. "Don't you ever take a day off?"

"The boss doesn't get to take a day off," Marco pointed out.

The boss. Maya's promotion was still new enough that she was getting used to it, just as she was getting used to thinking of Marco as Agent Spinelli rather than Detective Spinelli now that he'd gone through the FBI's training process.

Maya answered the call. As the head of her own department, she couldn't exactly ignore it, even on the weekend.

"Hi, Samit, what is it?" she asked, putting the phone on speaker.

"There's been another copycat."

"Another one?" Marco said. "That makes, what? Half a dozen since we caught him?"

"Eight, by my count, Agent Spinelli," Samit corrected him. "Although two of them were caught by local police, so we didn't have to get involved in the investigation."

Eight copycat killers, plus the work of trying to wind up the Moonlight Killer's network of dangerous contacts and unearth his many safehouses. Add to that new cold cases and the department that Maya now ran as a deputy director had quickly found itself busy.

Maya tried to consider what it was this time. "What do we have?"

"A woman's body found in Oregon. She was strangled with a ligature on the night of the full moon. The killer sent a postcard, demanding that the FBI try to hunt him down."

"Do local PD have any leads?" Marco asked.

"Nothing so far, but they called us pretty quickly. With the media coverage about the Moonlight Killer, they decided that it was connected right away."

That was happening more these days. Maya was starting to know how Agent Swift must have felt when any case remotely like the Moonlight Killer's handiwork had been sent over to her task force. Of course, none of it was Agent Swift's problem now that she'd moved over to run a department dealing with organized crime. Rumor around the office said that she was planning to make a run at becoming the head of the FBI when Adams retired.

Then there were the postcards. More and more killers seemed to be sending them in, copying this aspect of the Moonlight Killer's MO now that the full story had come out in the media.

None of that mattered right now, though. For now, Maya and Marco had to deal with this. They had another killer to chase.

"All right," Maya said. "We'll get into the office as soon as we can."

Maya hung up. She could see that Marco was already heading for the house to grab their go bags. Maya stood up and hugged her sister.

"It looks like we have to go," she said. She always had to go. There was always another case, always another killer, another copycat, another fragment of the Moonlight Killer's network.

As long as there were, though, Maya and Marco would be there, catching them—together.

NOW AVAILABLE!

ONCE HE SEES
(A Claire King FBI Suspense Thriller—Book One)

FBI Special Agent Claire King dies chasing a killer—and is resuscitated minutes later to realize she has changed. Dark images flash through her mind in a newfound power, visions leading her towards serial killers. But the riddles that plague her are obscured and conflicting, and Claire soon realizes that they may lead her to crack a case—or may just put her in the crosshairs of a killer.

"Molly Black has written a taut thriller that will keep you on the edge of your seat… I absolutely loved this book and can't wait to read the next book in the series!"
—Reader review for Girl One: Murder

Once He Sees is Book #1 of a long anticipated new series by critically-acclaimed and #1 bestselling mystery and suspense author Molly Black, whose books have received over 2,000 five-star reviews and ratings.

FBI Special Agent Claire King has a reputation for brilliance, for being able to crack serial killer cases that no other agent can. Before she died and came back to life, she relied solely on this brilliance. But now that she has this fleeting, newfound power, Claire is confused: should she follow what she knows? Or what she senses? Are visions more powerful than intellect?

Or will they lead her right into a killer's trap?

A page-turning and harrowing crime thriller featuring a brilliant and tortured FBI agent, the Claire King series is a riveting mystery, packed with non-stop action, suspense, twists and turns, revelations, and driven by a breakneck pace that will keep you flipping pages late into the night. Fans of Rachel Caine, Teresa Driscoll and Robert Dugoni are sure to fall in love.

Future books in the series are also available!

“I binge read this book. It hooked me in and didn't stop till the last few pages… I look forward to reading more!”
—Reader review for Found You

“I loved this book! Fast-paced plot, great characters and interesting insights into investigating cold cases. I can't wait to read the next book!”
—Reader review for Girl One: Murder

“Very good book… You will feel like you are right there looking for the kidnapper! I know I will be reading more in this series!”
—Reader review for Girl One: Murder

“This is a very well written book and holds your interest from page 1… Definitely looking forward to reading the next one in the series, and hopefully others as well!”
—Reader review for Girl One: Murder

“Wow, I cannot wait for the next in this series. Starts with a bang and just keeps going.”
—Reader review for Girl One: Murder

“Well written book with a great plot, one that will keep you up at night. A page turner!”
—Reader review for Girl One: Murder

“A great suspense that keeps you reading… can't wait for the next in this series!”
—Reader review for Found You

“Sooo soo good! There are a few unforeseen twists… I binge read this like I binge watch Netflix. It just sucks you in.”
—Reader review for Found You

Molly Black

Bestselling author Molly Black is author of the MAYA GRAY FBI suspense thriller series, comprising nine books (and counting); of the RYLIE WOLF FBI suspense thriller series, comprising six books; of the TAYLOR SAGE FBI suspense thriller series, comprising eight books; of the KATIE WINTER FBI suspense thriller series, comprising eleven books (and counting); of the RUBY HUNTER FBI suspense thriller series, comprising five books (and counting); of the CAITLIN DARE FBI suspense thriller series, comprising five books (and counting); of the REESE LINK mystery series, comprising five books (and counting); and of the CLAIRE KING mystery series, comprising five books (and counting).

An avid reader and lifelong fan of the mystery and thriller genres, Molly loves to hear from you, so please feel free to visit www.mollyblackauthor.com to learn more and stay in touch.

BOOKS BY MOLLY BLACK

MAYA GRAY MYSTERY SERIES
GIRL ONE: MURDER (Book #1)
GIRL TWO: TAKEN (Book #2)
GIRL THREE: TRAPPED (Book #3)
GIRL FOUR: LURED (Book #4)
GIRL FIVE: BOUND (Book #5)
GIRL SIX: FORSAKEN (Book #6)
GIRL SEVEN: CRAVED (Book #7)
GIRL EIGHT: HUNTED (Book #8)
GIRL NINE: GONE (Book #9)

RYLIE WOLF FBI SUSPENSE THRILLER
FOUND YOU (Book #1)
CAUGHT YOU (Book #2)
SEE YOU (Book #3)
WANT YOU (Book #4)
TAKE YOU (Book #5)
DARE YOU (Book #6)

TAYLOR SAGE FBI SUSPENSE THRILLER
DON'T LOOK (Book #1)
DON'T BREATHE (Book #2)
DON'T RUN (Book #3)
DON'T FLINCH (Book #4)
DON'T REMEMBER (Book #5)
DON'T TELL (Book #6)

KATIE WINTER FBI SUSPENSE THRILLER
SAVE ME (Book #1)
REACH ME (Book #2)
HIDE ME (Book #3)
BELIEVE ME (Book #4)

HELP ME (Book #5)
FORGET ME (Book #6)
HOLD ME (Book #7)
PROTECT ME (Book #8)
REMEMBER ME (Book #9)
CATCH ME (Book #10)
WATCH ME (Book #11)

RUBY HUNTER FBI SUSPENSE THRILLER
IF I RUN (Book #1)
IF I TELL (Book #2)
IF I LIVE (Book #3)
IF I FORGET (Book #4)
IF I RETURN (Book #5)

CAITLIN DARE FBI SUSPENSE THRILLER
COME GET ME (Book #1)
COME FIND ME (Book #2)
COME TAKE ME (Book #3)
COME CATCH ME (Book #4)
COME SAVE ME (Book #5)

REESE LINK MYSTERY
BEYOND REASON (Book #1)
BEYOND REACH (Book #2)
BEYOND REPAIR (Book #3)
BEYOND DOUBT (Book #4)
BEYOND NORMAL (Book #5)

CLAIRE KING MYSTERY
ONCE HE SEES (Book #1)
ONCE HE LONGS (Book #2)
ONCE HE TAKES (Book #3)
ONCE HE FEELS (Book #4)
ONCE HE KNOWS (Book #5)

Printed in Great Britain
by Amazon

58121753R00079